# Sport's Alien Fantasy

## A Novel by M. J. Scott
## With Daniel Wetta

Published by Daniel Wetta Publishing

Please visit authors on the website at
https://danielwetta.com/powersteeringus/

## Dedication

This journey is dedicated to the strong-hearted authors who search for creative word strength in defense of those who are weak or helpless. The highways described within this novel are peppered with intrigue and critical choices. May the reader feel the emotions that have been infused in Sport at every crossroad. If so, then her awareness and yours bring hope to our spinning planet.

# Table of Contents

# Prologue

*Virginia, 1962*

Years later, when Sport was thirty years old, she remembered the unique kindness of her first-grade art teacher who defended her in the year that she didn't feel safe. It was a memory that came top-of-mind to her whenever she puzzled about her dual memory stream, especially given that she was so scared when both her parents became unraveled and shouted at her, "You have to be out of your mind!" The impact of the incident upon Sport did not dawn upon her until after the bus accident that marked the sudden turn of her life. She was just a little girl, but her parents planted an idea in her that she was crazy.

She wanted to please them to change their opinion of her. Things did not go much better at school. The first-grade teacher seemed to have a dubious assessment of Sport as well. It wasn't what she said to Sport. It was how nervous she made Sport's stomach feel.

In a way, it was the art teacher's encouragement that incited Sport's natural tendency to effervescence and energy. Sport could see the affection that this teacher had for her in her red-haired, freckly smiles. She had never seen anyone else in the mountains with her own hair color and complexion, and, for that reason, Sport felt at ease with this fun person of instruction since day one.

"You showed me how to cut pretty paper and use paste to make things," Sport cried in a trembling pout the next day at school after the incident of parental explosion. "My daddy was decorating with wall paper, and when he was gone, I put up some paper to help him. I wanted to surprise him. But they told me I messed up the wall and that I mess up everything and that I am not a good girl because I don't have good thoughts sometimes. They told me they want to take me to see a doctor about my mind."

Alone with Ms. Swanson in the art room, Sport rushed to the sweet lady's calming arms. Her teacher hugged her close until she stopped crying.

"Aw, gentle Sport, I think maybe your parents had a bad day and they just yelled, honey," the teacher comforted. "But you know what? When I was a little girl, I was always in trouble, too, because of my imagination. We red-heads just have lots of funny mischief in us that people need time to get used to. Didn't you know this?"

"No," Sport admitted. No one had ever told her something like that before.

"Well, putting up wall paper is hard work, and it has to be done perfectly, or bubbles appear in it. It's a grown-up job that is not possible even for some grown-ups. You just didn't know this."

"No, I didn't," Sport answered. Her chest had stopped heaving from the sobs. "But I am scared to tell them things because they act funny with me when I do. I never told them about my dreams about the people who died. Well, I'm not sure if they are dreams or real, because I still see them and remember."

Ms. Swanson took Sport's arms and extended her backwards so that she could see her face. Sport saw her tender smile, but she also saw the questioning in her eyes. She had tried to tell her parents a couple of times before, but they didn't look comfortable at all, and, shortly after the last time, they began using that expression that she was out of her mind. Now she wasn't sure whether Ms. Swanson knew what to do with this news.

"What do you mean, sweetie? Who died?"

"They couldn't breathe," Sport said. "Everything was okay in the..." She looked up at her art teacher and saw the puzzlement on her face. "I don't remember," she said, and the teacher's expression relaxed somewhat. Her art teacher was the only person who didn't seem to find her annoying, and she didn't want to lose the safe feeling with her. Most of the time, when Sport tried to think of the dream, she couldn't quite bring back what it was about. In Ms. Swanson's arms that morning, however, she remembered some things in vivid detail.

They had left the place of bright colors a long time ago. She remembered seeing through a window the circle that kept getting smaller. There were grownups in the rooms with her most of the time, always busy with the lights and the machines. They talked a lot, but nothing stuck in her memory about what they said.

*Until they got excited and said they had flown too close to the star that stole their energy.*

There was a lady whom Sport kept getting confused with her mother on the few occasions that she could recall some of these details.

2

*Why did we come here?* Sport thought she had asked once. She noted that the woman had been crying.

*We were coming to help because their time has come,* said the woman's voice. *They are shooting things into the void. Some are good. Some are bad, like in our ancient days.*

One day the word came to Sport's mind when she was with Ms. Swanson, so she asked her what "ancient" meant. Ms. Swanson laughed and told her that it meant "very old." Her teacher looked at Sport curiously and said to her, "Sport, if your mother will let you, why don't you and I go on a picnic up on the mountain Saturday?" Sport was thrilled. The teacher saw her mother later that afternoon, and the special time with Ms. Swanson was set.

When they got out of the car, her teacher took Sport's hand, and they went to a path that ambled beside a gurgling stream and began to ascend. Ms. Swanson stopped at intervals for them to catch breath. On one of the breaks, she asked, "So tell me, Sport, what do you want to be when you grow up?"

"A school teacher, " Sport replied quickly. "I want to help people like you do."

They came to a point on the path that had a clearing on the left that offered a view of the valley and neighboring mountains. On the right of the path was the steep, vertical ascent of the mountain that they were on. Something about the vista in that particular place and the moist smell of humidity on Sport's skin triggered a dream-memory that Sport was unsure whether she had experienced or not.

She saw the people from the journey lying motionless among the trees, except for one or two who struggled with breathing. The one that she confused with her mother raised her head slightly, trying to answer Sport's questions. Sport suddenly had an overwhelming feeling of suffocation.

*There is not quite enough oxygen here*, the woman said weakly to Sport.

The dream-memory was making Sport skittish. She ran to Ms. Swanson. "I can't breathe!" she told her. In the arms of her teacher, she remembered the attack of panic that she had experienced earlier that winter. The doctor had come to the house.

"When Sport can't breathe, she goes into absolute panic," said her mother.

"She needs more oxygen," the doctor replied. "You have it too stuffy in her room. I myself am hot in your home. When Sport has trouble breathing and gets upset, open the windows in her room so she can get more air."

Ms. Swanson had sat on a log, and Sport had climbed into her lap. The two were quiet until Sport's breathing became regular and peaceful. Then Ms. Swanson said to her, "Are you okay, honey? I think maybe you have some kind of asthma or allergy. Does this happen to you often?"

"Yes, ma'am," replied Sport.

"Okay, well, we will just sit here until you are ready and we can talk. Later, we'll go back to the car and get our picnic basket and eat at that table area we saw. How does that sound?"

"Great! I'm hungry!"

Ms. Swanson laughed. She stroked Sport's curly, red hair.

Sport thought about what she had seen on television the previous night. A rocket had been counting down to lift off. They had played what President Kennedy had once said, that the United States would be the first to put a man on the moon. When the rocket began its climb, Sport saw the brightest light she had ever seen issue behind it, and then the light followed the rocket into the sky as if it were pushing it.

It was like the light that confused all her memories.

# Introduction: Planetary Life

Sport felt like she was drowning as she left the birth canal, too tiny to swim, but determined to scream right into the bright shining of life. A red-headed, green-eyed, noisy little monster, she was born into a room with all white walls and figures peering at her.

*Well, Sport, you have the spotlight, and you are baby number one!*

It didn't seem that more activity was required. She squirmed in a warm blanket and closed her eyelids again. There seemed to be comfort coming from the arms holding her, and then came the thing called a crib. The arms of the little bed were not warm; she was in a tiny cell.

*Better figure out what this life is like. This is very strange from where I have been!*

A murmur of voices surrounded her, clearer than those she had heard before, but in a language that she had not learned. The beings applied to her feet soft booties and then the warm cover of a blanket. She felt warm again. She learned later that it was November, but her primal sense of time was a season of lifting, bouncing and hearing strange roars. No angels had prepared her for the chill and noise.

*What have I gotten into*, she wondered as her brain tried to bridge the past with now. Sirens and town noises accompanied her ride to a different white environment. It smelled good. Sport fell asleep on her third day of emergence into the new world, and then followed awakening to more sounds and voices and peering faces. There came a needle to make her feel good.

*Whoops! No, not so good. This sensation of feeling on earth could have unpleasantness that she had not experienced before.*

There was a blur of time, and later she learned that two years had passed. The interval seemed like a nothingness between the needle prick and the wetness of an animal tongue. That came accompanied by a whiny singing and whimpering. The puppy licked her fingers and discovered her tears. Sometimes, she barely recalled a memory of brightly covered vegetation and fragrant, thick air, and she couldn't hold on to it. She didn't think that it belonged to the two-year interval period. It seemed more a near-glimpse of someplace before her time, before her emergence on earth.

After the puppy appeared a loving, freckled-faced person with red hair. Sport wondered after he kissed her: *Maybe I belong to him? What was that warm touch of the lips?* A nice sensation, and a first memory to pack away of her grandfather. Then smiled a pretty woman with long black hair. Reaching down from her white quilts, she accepted Sport from a figure in a white uniform. Lifting Sport to the bed, the pretty woman smiled and stroked her hand. Again came a kiss of warm belonging. This was the beautiful angel, Grandma. She felt like she had known love like this before.

The noise of cars chugging down the street soon became replaced by a sudden quiet except for the sound of the wind in the tall Australian pine. Well, that's what she was told it was when later she admired it stretching toward the sky.

A time skip, and then…

An explosion! A scream, and all of them raced down the hall, away from Sport. They hurried in a panic to a dark place that blazed with red light. The maid had poured kerosene on the coal embers to light the furnace, and Sport's grandfather had rushed into the blaze to extinguish the fire and save the house. Sport's next memories were the sounds of grieving - a loud sadness that terrified her. Her puppy, the Newfie, began with her at that time the deep bond of friendship that lasted years. She and the dog became inseparable. His friendship carried her past the silence of the parlor into the days ahead and scents of flowers. That explosion had taken her cherished grandfather away. No more the cuddling in his lap as he sang. Sport felt another skip of time to a strange silence that permeated the huge colonial home in the country. It was a period of more flowers and flooding tears. Grandma was gone too!

After these two heartbreaks, a closet of short time held happiness and play. The doll arrived. She had black hair, brown eyes and made a lot of noise. Sport was told that this was her new baby sister. There had been no warning that she was going to have a new playmate. The other dolls had been quiet and had only opened and shut their eyes. However, this new item could cry and wiggle. Sport was assigned to watch the little sleeping burden and to call when it opened its eyes. Mother had never given her a task like that with her dolls or with Lassie, her Newfie. So, while baby sister snoozed in her crib in the afternoons in the west room, Sport cuddled Lassie, and he rested his head upon her arm.

6

*Wow, this life is getting busier!*

Then one day the tall handsome man, her father, came and took her puppy away. She pleaded with him, "Why can't Lassie stay?" His explanation that she was suffering and needed to find an angel home was no comfort.

A deep empty feeling wiggled its way into Sport's chest, forming a lump of emotional longing and loss that seeped into all her tiny molecular cells. In her memory, she coped by becoming a time and space traveler on adventures to find her dog.

The doll grew quickly. Her little sister would sit all fluffy and pretty in the swing. Once, Sport got to push her, and with every return, Sport would send her a little higher. The pretty pink dress went flying right out of the swing. A crying little sister in flight; a crying Sport in punishment. There seemed to be a sentence of not belonging. Sport cried herself to sleep, and a closet of darkness engulfed her like the night outside her window, but with no stars to cheer her weary red eyes.

Then one Sunday when the scent of lilacs surfed a southern breeze, Sport's daddy said, "Let's go for a walk in the orchard." They walked from the front porch through the little gate just beyond the end of the driveway. They walked past the chicken-breeder houses where the sounds of little chicks crept through the screens. The meandering stream was a welcome surprise as this was her first introduction to the orchard. The grass in the orchard tickled Sport's legs as she trotted beside her father. She gasped in wonder at the apple trees. *Are they for climbing?* Farther along came the three large cherry trees. *Wow, they look good for climbing too!*

Their walk brought them to a little fairyland heaven so undisturbed that it was only shared with a floor of purple violets. There they found a waiting log for sitting and resting. Conversations were rare for this tall handsome man, her Daddy. He said, "It's here in the spring that the Indians used to come and get their water." There was a softness in his voice, almost a celestial reverence for an earlier time. To Sport, fascinated by the violets and the sounds of the bubbling spring, arrived a mind-searching question: *Who were these people, and did they have children who played in the soft green moss?*

Jumping for joy, Sport bolted away from her Daddy and leapt across the stream and ended with wet feet and mud-splattered dress.

*What will Mother say,* Sport worried. Just yesterday her mother had warned her about wearing five dresses in one day. That was just too many. Her mother had washed the dresses by hand in a tub on the back porch, and then they looked pretty blowing in the Saturday breeze. But there were other dress temptations: The spring chicks were so fluffy yellow, and they loved to cuddle in her lap. Sport would stroke their fuzz. She found their little chirps so endearing. *Well, another dress today, but not really that dirty!*

Everyone, even the live-in nurse, Georgia, tried to take care of Sport and little sister. Georgia always went up and down the back stairs to a room never explored by Sport. *Sometime I will,* she thought. When Sport had a pounding, heart-beat earache, the doctor came from town to see her. Through the pain and fever she heard him murmur, "We'll have to operate here. Georgia will hold her tight." A strange lump behind Sport's left ear was causing the pain. Numbness and silence were the results after the doctor lanced the lump, installed a bandage, and left the old house. Later the throbbing pain gave way to healing, leaving only a tiny scar behind the ear as a reminder.

She began to realize that Daddy was away a lot. *What now?* Breakfast was never spent with all of them together - Daddy, Mother, Georgia, little sister and Sport. Sport learned to play with her sniffly two-year-old sister. They loved to make mud pies on the big stone step that introduced the walk up to the porch. The stone had strange shapes, like ripples of water.

*What fun!* But a question insisted in Sport's mind: Why were these strange and beautiful shapes there? Mother had explained that during the Glacial Age the lines were carved by ice. They were called glacial grooves. *Wow!*

The family farm was huge. It had a towering hill running along the skyline beyond the barn bank. She later learned another geology lesson, that she was living on the very edge of mountains pushed up to form the Appalachian Plateau.

A new dog, Lady, sometimes joined the playmates, but usually she was in the barn as governess of the grain bin, hay loft and pigeons. Sport overheard her parents say, "We can't let her out, as people will think she is a black bear. Besides, we don't want any unexpected puppies." (*What? What does that mean?*) It turned out to be Sport's first lesson about sex. Sport realized that interesting

8

lessons often came from listening to conversations that little ears perhaps were not supposed to hear. In their elegant home, they were living somewhat a Victorian lifestyle, Sport later concluded.

When Auntie and Sport's two little girl cousins came to visit, wisps of words created occasional intrigues. Their family lived in town in a little white house. Sport questioned the gorgeous woodwork in her house. Why were there large columns that seemed to melt into the casing and flow like a wooden ripple? She learned that skilled carpenters from England had built the house. That made her wonder about her great-grandfather's house. How many had come (and from where) to build it? Oh, breathless wonder when a leak in family history revealed that their farm was a land grant from the King! Ancestors: A big word from a far country, and the builders had arrived from Scotland and Ireland!

Sport believed that a looming place called "school" might tell her more. Well, five years old was coming. She found out that she would go there in the big yellow egg carton that she had seen. She did know about eggs. There were bunches of eggs in cages in their basement. Then along came the peeping surprises. No wonder Sport loved the chicks! This meant, of course, several dresses would always be hanging on the clothesline connecting the rambling porch and the maple tree.

Just so much to learn! Cousins up on the hill came to visit and asked if they could take Sport to see the high school. *High school must mean that it's high off the ground,* Sport surmised. Sure enough, when they arrived there, the ascending cement steps left her breathless. The hallway full of kids racing down the steps became crowded after the sudden ringing of a bell. Her cousins grabbed Sport's hand and pulled her out of the way. She felt the warmth of flesh as she brushed the big kids' legs. Sport's sensitive ears hurt as long as the bell rang. It was a real fire. Outside, they gathered on a big field that sloped to a creek. Sport wondered if this strange place was for her. But the inviting swings and teeter-tot reassured her that the place was not so bad, after all.

September brought the egg carton to her driveway. She struggled to climb the steps through its doors. The driver was an old friend who knew her mom. They had gone to school together. His warm hand engulfed Sport's trembling one and melted her fears. She caught the smell of the gasoline as the bus (now its real name and purpose were known) left the gravel driveway. Sport saw her apple and cherry trees disappearing from the view of the back window.

Up another gravel lane – kind of narrow for such a big bus – and it made stops for a few kids along the way to the village. Her cousins led Sport to a strange room. She was placed in the back row of desks. Sport was tall for her age, and the teacher had arranged the students' seat assignments by height. But Sport couldn't see the blackboard up front, so she had to stand up to see whatever those odd shapes were. *This is a not so great new experience.* But she could discern colorful, pretty letter shapes lining the rim around the ceiling because those were close to her.

In fact, those became the fun things for her. With paper and pencil, Sport got to draw what the teacher called, "letter people." But glee was short-lived. The teacher, all plump in her long dress, gave the sixteen students hard lessons by putting the letter people to work. She said, "See Dick! See Jane!" Sport had no liking for Dick and Jane, and seeing the dog run was much more fun when Lady did it. Sport learned the pictures in the book, and the teacher thought that she could read. The pictures were the clues to deciphering the strange word forms. *Ouch!* Having learned to be a good listener, Sport memorized the entire book. And the second book as well. The dog was running faster now. At the end of the second book, there was a list of words without pictures. That complicated things.

The teacher wasn't happy with Sport's performance. She sent her home with additional assignments to learn the alien word forms. Daddy was upset. Mother was irritated, too. They were paying for Sport to go to school, but now they had to teach her how to read. That must have been a hidden challenge, because, years later, Sport learned that her mother had to quit school at the end of sixth grade because her family needed her to work. Daddy had done slightly better: He made it through seventh grade.

Somehow the reading obstacle got overcome, but Sport was still sitting in the back row of seats. She still had to stand or sit on the edge of her desk to discern the teacher's lettering on the blackboard. Despite her protests that she couldn't see, she was scolded once in humiliating fashion in front of her classmates for standing. Tears of frustration welled and cascaded down Sport's face. The teacher bodily rushed her out of the classroom. In the dark corridor, Sport saw a man approaching with outstretched hand.

*Maybe he will understand!* He lifted his hand, but it was not the hand of comfort like the bus driver's. Instead, he twisted Sport around and paddled her for bad classroom behavior. Oh, this hurt drilled right to the very core of Sport's being. And worse, there was anticipation of another whipping to come at home.

But first grade didn't end just with that indignity. Clouds seemed to press in on Sport as learning accumulated. The teacher believed in teaching with visible objects. The first was a shoestring. That was easy, just a little hard to form the tie and hold in place. "Practice makes perfect," said the teacher. Buttons also were no problem.

But then came the Friday morning lesson, a zipper. The teacher showed one with steel-tooth meshing that looked like jaws. Sport had never noticed one before, so at home the assignment was to find a zipper. That was not so easy, as it wasn't in Mother's sewing basket or her wet washed clothes.

That evening Daddy came home. After dinner, he did a rare thing and said, "Sport, come sit on my lap and tell me about school." This was during a time when Sport was still learning those hard words with no pictures at the end of the book. Out of the blue, Sport spotted Daddy's zipper, and she realized that it would go down like the teacher had shown them. She could do her assignment! Her quick fingers attached to her homework in delight. But suddenly there was a shout of rejection, and she was dumped to the floor. What had she done wrong? Tears ensued, and there were no loving hands for her that night. First grade had felt torturous. What would second grade bring?

An art teacher was teaching them about colors and water. What fun to discover that colors didn't have to be contained in a coloring box! Sport poured her little soul into this new-found expression of art. Maybe this was hers to enjoy! The little blue lunch box had lost its fascination. These lessons went smoothly, and experimentation was Sport's little joy. Reading was still a chore.

At home, new wall paper had rushed to little eager hands, and Sport was allowed an after-school brush with the color pictures on a small section of the wall. She got to help finish the last by smoothing the bubbles after the pasting. What a fun thing! Before dinner, her parents went to the barn to finish the milking. Little sister was playing on the kitchen carpet. Sport got a little pan of water and fished her fingers through the liquid. She made a splash on the wallpaper of apples, peaches, pears and grapes. These had become dull in the late afternoon. *Oh, Mommy and Daddy will be so proud of me, making them all bright again!* Splish, splash, a high fling, and even the ceiling seemed to be laughing! Art was a love that Sport had found in the kitchen wallpaper. Her childhood glee was complete.

Having finished the chores, her tired parents came in with the warm cow milk ready for cooling. They were met with an all-wet Sport, a messy floor and the wallpaper laughing in beautiful, peeling colors. Sport was about to get a lesson in big words. "You've lost your mind," her parents screamed! Out came the leather shaving belt from behind the door. Dad's lashing penetrated her flesh right into Sport's soul. This was much worse than the paddling at school or any previous one at home. In an instant, a giant stroke of anger changed everything. Sport cried herself to sleep alone that night. She had received a big taste of life, and now she hated milk. It curdled her stomach like cottage cheese. *Yuck!*

Yet, country-school lessons and home-school lessons were merging to forge a more strong-willed Sport.

Reading came easier in second grade, but then writing became another skill to perfect. A German handwriting teacher taught the method that everyone should be able to print with a penny on top of their hand. When pennies fell to the floor, it meant a chide as she walked the room with a ruler. Pennies abounded on the hardwood second-grade floor, while up in front of the classroom George Washington and Abraham Lincoln watched, never smiling approval of the writing efforts.

Recess was not easy on the bundled-up cold days. The swings were for the big kids, and they flew high. Sport had a jolting memory of little sister in aerial flight. She raced for the sliding board, but its cold steel slide never felt like a good choice.

But always the merry-go-round had kids to play with! Someone lifted her up to it, but as it went faster and faster, Sport felt a tummy-urge to leave it all behind. She wanted to get off this laughing, funny, whirling machine that others were loving. When she attempted to jump off, her leg caught in a hold grip, and she got dragged in cold sand a few whirls as others tried to stop it. She had a red, dripping gash in her right leg, not something soon to forget.

The playground seemed more like a grim ground to Sport, so after a few days at recess, she started to walk toward the village's tall lamps. She got all the way to the bridge where she saw that the water was all red like the blood from the merry-go-round misadventure. A teacher caught up with Sport, the little runaway.

*But it wasn't running away! It was exploring!*

Sport saw by the teacher's expression that parental involvement would be coming.

Her parents were horrified by the mortuary doing the dead man's drop in the river and by Sport's behavior which had led her there.

That night, Sport's upset stomach shot bands of pain that kept her awake into the small hours. But as the silence of the pre-dawn calmed the countryside, Sport released the anxieties that had stoked the pains. She drifted, finally, into a sleep that felt like dreaming wakefulness. She saw a city of silos surrounded by vast fields of waving grains and a sunrise that lit up an ocean-green sky. A young boy appeared and spoke to her and told her his name was Tommy. When she awoke in the morning, she wanted to cling to that world of joy, but its vivid imagery faded into a grey blur of forgetting.

# Section One: Ascent

# Chapter 1: Sport's Alien Fantasy

Sport valued her own thoughts and feelings, and she tuned to her inner messages. Her heart named her, calling her, "Messenger." Her mind grasped this meaning of self. She came to the urgent feeling of seeking a special place where she felt understood, recognized and loved.

She intuited that she was a unique person who wore a fragile veil of sensitivity rarely refined on planet earth. She didn't know why, but she would find out. From the deep of her, an inner silence sang, released not with lips but with sensors from an indwelling foreign spirit. This other life source flowed from her in rivers of expression. When Sport felt the force of its current, she could not contain it. She favored an advice to others: *Inhale the deep wonder of the secret unfolding. In wondering, the universe reveals mystery to you!*

Sport's niche of abilities began to deepen. She discovered new views of the world. She saw moonlight as pale as the blue gown of early morning's touch. It was a trace of light, but with a wonderfully haunting aura that transformed everything in the world. The beauty of her nights lied embraced in the peace of crickets' choruses. Moments blended harmoniously. She sometimes felt balanced on a tip of time on some frail and fragile planet. She had an urging desire to be transported back before the beginning of time when she would know all secrets hidden from memory's vaults and eyes' pleading dances. Sport would seek her senses, keen for clues to understanding the karmic past. She knew that it unwinds in the present, and she was always fascinated by its impulses in the today!

She would wonder, *"How will tomorrow allow itself to be seen and remembered?"* She looked ahead into a grey area of life, a remnant of the faint twilight of the past. Sport would close her eyes in deep thought and meditation. Motionless. Quiet. One looking at her then would see her countenance and perceive the lovely face that laughed through eyes and mouth. She cared deeply for humanity whom she thought of as "dear people."

Sometimes, in deep meditation, she took herself to another world. She fancied that she constructed it in her imagination, but the truth that this came so easily to her nagged her consciousness. She liked to meet the people of the other world, and she delighted when one would become her partner for the evening. Often, she sat with a special one of her friends under evening skies of changing colors. He was a handsome young man who liked to look at her. Sport knew that she was in love with him because his gaze enraptured her and promised to steal her next breath. When this became too intense for Sport, she would select a different friend for the evening.

The special one told her that his name was Tommy. He could be enthusiastically chatty, and he liked to regale Sport with his tales of life in silo cities. But one evening, Sport wanted to see him from afar, just to watch and admire him furtively. She caught him when he was talking with a friend about her! She sat still as a grassland rabbit when humans walked near. Tommy was explaining to his friend:

"These are things that Sport tells me while I look at her. She is so beautiful that I cannot remove my eyes! There is a halo of light that bends under her eyelids. She sees a new dimension. It is a gift from the deep past, arriving from a time-distance of light years. The light changes shapes. Sport perceives a ball, then a roadway. She feels as if she is in a dream, and she sees ladders of extension. The clouds separate and make new forms. An island rises to its height. A steppingstone pathway of light illuminates the way for its newcomer. She makes her way through ice crystals, past castles of miniature design, and takes in the sky's created jewelry.

"All these pictures that she sees… Sport measures them in units of beauty as they trace memories upon her heart. She says her video-mind retains everything in indelible technicolor. I see her face is aglow with the gentleness that blesses her, but her gentleness is also the boundlessness of her strength.

"Once she spoke about her birth like this: 'The beauty of the heavens is swallowed by tiny forceps. I don't want to go. My divergent mind clings to the sights of misty clouds seeking the remaining light. Is that another moon, or native lore, changing myths, thoughts, or seasons seen in translucent light? *Just another hour, please.*

"Clouds in the heavens become a mirror that reflects the loveliness of Sport and her yearning. She remains in the quiet place, as if she were sitting in distant mountains that were her private haven for tuning in to the main channel of purpose. *What is this purpose? Where is this place?* she wonders. Sport sees very few seeking to

16

understand contentment. They miss a peace unbent by human hands. They attempt to erase great discords of life.

"I see her leaning forward, toward the open window of wisdom. She sees a new dimension forming, looking like a pink cloud glowing as it rolls one and a half times to encircle the eye of night. In this dimension, she understands time. Time is the kindness of a voice saying, 'Hello there!' It passes the person accepted and loved, like the wind free in its journey, when no freedom is taken and nothing is asked. It is the movement of the caring voice that gives a portion of self, even in the most frenetic paces of time."

Tommy's assessment of her thrilled Sport's heart. She jumped up from her yoga mat and accepted the rude inhale of earthly air. He was gone, yet she imagined his smell from the times when he was close to her.

She took a step and sighed. It was the top step of the stairs to a day's rest coming the next day. She comforted herself: *The tomorrow nearing holds promise of newness and another journey into fulfillment. Day has turned into night as the wind rises.*

Sport's world tilted to a brightened pearl of luster in the full-moon night. She walked to her porch. Like a magnet, she was attracted to the clouds that jetted away before her penetrating eyes. An arrowhead cloud tore the sky in its aim to the sought-after.

It was a night of autumn sky, an indigo ocean with radio waves overpowering the frequencies of starlight. Filled with wonder, her pulse raced with excitement. In the moonglow of light, she felt the piercing of a new understanding: In this outer vision, she was witnessing the birth of some new life for her. Her being was tuning to harmony, peace and abundant love.

Looking upward, she released a contented sigh. *That full-moon beauty is the rare Indian-summer night when leaves are expecting change but hold on to continue yet another day. The leaves cling as in every year, ageless in time, in colors for earth. I feel the breezes of radio waves. This is explained by the flutter of angels' wings above the earth, where man races and roars noisily. But I am the searching, vibrating, sensing alien, Sport, a quiet alpha-null in a shadow of time. Whatever thoughts I project as images get tangled in the tree branches, which reshape them into new pictures. Some keep, and some disappear.*

Like Sport. She disappeared into her peaceful meditation of the night sky and went to a different place.

Different! Yes, for the visions of night still lingered after the whole day gone. Alien heart sat breathless on a curb of dreams at the stoplight, where she found great pieces of machinery turning her corner. She felt glued to her curbside seat, able to move only a fraction of space. A giant iron of massive steel bore down close to her. The heat of its breath exhausted her instantly, and the booms of its activity passed just above her head. She felt her security threatened, but at the same time, she recalled recurring dreams of even stranger machines that created wonder in her ancestral memory. *It is a revelation: machines of great proportions will eventually lift my life from stationary places of dreamlike curbs. It is a promise of new journeys in high machines. Alien fantasy, is there more?*

Music floated into Sport's hearing. Her breathing slackened. She partook another relaxing moment. She realized that she could adapt easily to the transitions of living, listening or dreaming. In this moment, she noticed that she was listening to two tracks simultaneously: one of listening to another speaker and the other being the music permeating her mind. Oh, the seconds to achieve the singular focus necessary to examine her deepest feelings and thoughts! She felt like a stranger in a roomy world, but then population crept into her territory of awareness. In the distance, Sport saw the beauty of a bridge that was holding apart the banks of the stream flowing below, as clouds drifted on its mirror surface. Hers was a different view from that of the sad person sitting on the river bank. He had gone there to escape the crowds and to reflect on his loneliness.

There was a special place of rest that Sport loved. Her thoughts drifted there, from her seacoast to the mountain range, over a farther range, and then to the western shore. Words cut into Sport's imagining; they changed her thoughts and provoked different dimensions of creativity. *What is it I am supposed to create*, she wondered. *Is it a new concept of life beyond this pearl of night, not here in this moment, but somewhere in the hereafter?* The hereafter would become the "now" of her life, and she would leave behind the others in the before. They would not comprehend her unique position and mission. For Sport, the tunnel of creative thought only ran forward, but she knew that there was another road running in parallel. *Well, at least one,* she thought. *How many roads have I traversed?* She wished everyone would think about the paths they were on and how many they had traveled.

She remembered some more words of Tommy to his friend. He saw things about her, and this made her love him insanely.

*Sport is a night person. She finds her inner energies higher on the night points of the clock. It is how she is structured. The quiet hours are her growing moments, out of the way of the day mowers that constantly clip the potential of peace. She knows that there are some others like her, aliens of heart who may never meet but who share the same intimate needs - special people who linger in thought but rarely in proximity. Like birds loving to be free, they are off to new borders to seek answers to questions that form in those places. Their hope is for enlightenment.*

Sport slipped beneath her quilt and curled up in her space-like fetal shape for a moment. Instant warmth returned in the safety of this protecting place. The myriad of thoughts continued to impose pictures in her busy brain. These didn't slow the sorting, computing processes with which Sport evaluated the events of life and worked to solve the great puzzle of its meaning.

She had a revelation about myths: Sport thought that myths are moments spun together in story form to celebrate the splendor of mystical events that would otherwise go unsung were it not for the story tellers. The myths accrued layers as the moments of life accelerated. To reverse the pace of life would unravel the myths, and all would be out of step with time.

Sport's mind said, *Where have all these deep thoughts and royally framed concepts originated? Ah, the heart of creativity is the Creator. Each cell of His creative life implants in man, who must discover his path of origin. The stardust of creation blinds man, however; even deep space puts men of high vision into distracted trances. They can become lost in the murky depths of unawareness. It requires a physical search for the emotional, spiritual and mental components that fit together to form the total man, the complete being who sees clearly into the beyond. The fog and obscurity of distorted reality clouds the search. Let the sigh escape! Let the restraining inertia of life in a busy world lose its grip!*

Sport stretched beneath her quilt. She wondered the whereabouts of all the aliens of the planet. Someone searching for her, some dreamer, might find that she was the stars in his eyes, or the wonder in a sunrise, or the unknown in his being. *If I am alien,* Sport thinks, *then maybe I am neither male nor female. On a rare night like this, I know who I am. I know who we are. We are the hope beyond the valley of effort. To forget us would mark an incomplete life. To search for us leads to discovery of the gifts that are the core of each vibrant life.*

Her thoughts flew like light waves. She wanted to share them. She had an urgent need for a companion, but there was no one to turn to at that hour. *I will create him,* she decided. She imagined someone she could talk to, someone who would wonder where they fit in time and space and would ask her.

She said to him, "The ultimate truth is that everyone can delve into the substance of themselves to discover what they are, what they have been, and what they are to become. We must not fail the real person we are in our soul, the leeward or wayward, that is neither full nor empty, neither left nor right, nor up or down. We feel a forceful urge to be, to become, and to be understood."

Her companion looked slightly puzzled but comfortable in her presence. A welcoming warmth made them both relax. Something or someone was with them. So gentle in its arriving, so comforting, so unexplainably beautiful in its encompassing freedom. Sport felt like her listener would understand. She told him, "Climb out from the encumbering hours of your physical life into this new wave of relief. If someone claims it has a name, then from the unnamed it becomes known. Look above the walls of so-called reality to the realms of wonder, thought and dream. There you will sense the Creator, who exists outside of time and who inspires us to search for perfection, but it is a perfection of knowing ourselves and our relationship to the Creator. This is possible only if we truly relax. Relaxing is a rare state in chemical processes, but the physical rhythms of dimensions beyond bring it to us."

Sport's imaginary companion asked her about this relaxation, this peace, whether it was like the lofty spiraling of a leaf downward after its departure from a tree's far heights. The leaf's lightness of being occurs when the tree has let go. Sport told him that the peace is like unexplored vastness, like Antarctica in its size, but deeper than deep and farther than away.

"The peace has no shape," she says, "and it asks for no house to contain it. When you give yourself to it, you are simply a unit of the Totality. You are part of the synthesis of all being."

The chill stung like early winter, and the flickering fire made the fireplace of home a sheltered haven. Sport's thoughts danced quickly away, extracting questions of strange times and lands. A sudden revelation caused her to lean on a chair for support. She caught her breath. It was a wild floor-side dream providing strange insight into life in the past. It made her question the ages of ice and glacial changes. She could almost feel the glacial grooves in the stone she had rubbed with her hands as a child. She remembered the rocks that had ripples etched by water. Did Ice Age man come from her far away home? Were these generations now all her people? Alien from the universe they had left and had never returned, were they alien like her here?

Later, as she thought about all of this, the rest of the memory about what happened returned to her. That night the mystery of those things seemed hidden in the fire and in the cackling of the wood. Sport had chosen to undertake the journey of the mind and to experience distant yearnings. *Can I comprehend the majesty and magnitude of it all,* she wondered?

Her imaginary companion reminded her of his presence once again. *That is good*, she thought, *I need dialog.*

She wanted an anchor of someone present, because, although she no longer felt a stranger to herself or to the universe, she was forging ahead of her time into the known of the supposedly unknown. She was riding an expansion of the present moment like an explorer going to the distant past and future. She wanted to share her new-found treasure of knowledge, and her companion was there, observing it all.

"This dancing fire, so important now, will be gone in the morning," she told him. "The greatest time is the now. It is always the most sensitive. And in the now, the greatest meaning is love. Love holds the deepest feeling in beauty that words fail to express. Everyone tries to capture its nature with words in poetry, sonnet, story and song. Sometimes touch expresses it better, or the meeting of eyes or the tenderness of voice."

Sport grabbed a quickened breath. She felt the melting of her companion's defenses. He was sending positive waves, the harbinger of love. She could read his eyes like other people read printed words on pages. She could grasp his sentiments by the turn of his lip or the traces of his smile or frown. The energy of her vivaciousness, the luster of her personality, the spectral colors of her feelings disarmed the emotional defenses of her friend. He surrendered to her all his information. This was true with everyone that she met.

Her companion asked her if she were human or a computer. It wasn't a question about the presence or absence of feelings; rather, its purpose was to understand the rapidity of her assessments.

"I think I am human in my form," she explained, "but my ability to synthesize and process the whole of any situation seems like an alien ability. By that I mean extra-human. I am more than a computer. A computer can chart an expectation from a programmed incident, but I add dimensions and temperature and create emotion and attitude. I absorb intangible vibrations beyond the sender's awareness of transmission. It is as if I have antennae to receive these transmissions and relay them for almost instant comprehension."

Sport saw that he was digesting what she had said. She possessed a self-awareness that she sometimes experienced a kind of alien fantasy, one in which she combined the wisdom of the past with the attuned sensitivity of life in the now. It came upon her like a flash of blinding light. The past and present would join at an unexpected crossroads to become a heightened encounter. She hoped that her companion might see what was happening. She hoped that he could read between the lines of her explanations for a deeper understanding.

*He must be feeling something*, she thought, because then he asked her, "Where do these wild combinations form?"

"They form in the subliminal reservoir of the inner person. Each of us is capable of drilling for its contents so that an elevated level of meaning can flow into our mainstream of thought. It takes much experience to develop alertness to the greatness beneath our epidermis. Sometimes I hear the crashing waves of the excitement in me. I think the discernment I experience arrives to me from beyond man and time, coming from the very core of life, something we describe as soul, a precious core that can store the gifts of comprehension. Within each of us, in soul, lies truth, the marrow of knowledge."

"Tell me a story," her companion said.

Sport had a flash that his shift of conversation was meant to test her and that his request was designed to evoke not only a truth, but a memory.

*Oh, he is clever. He reminds me to communicate with tangible concepts that people can grasp,* she thought.

It worked. There came the blinding flash of light and the bells ringing in Sport's brain.

She remembered that she and her brother had seen each other. She began describing it to her companion.

"We began to talk, and the talking seemed to never cease. It was as if our yearnings vibrated at the same frequency. We never really spoke of who we were or whether we would meet again. And it ended in a moment. Our sharing of lives was over. He has a name, but I understood him as an alien brother on a coast far away. In my soul, I know that I met him in the distant past. He was gifted in reading my mind or the touch of my hand or my eyes. It was unnerving to me to grasp this, being unprepared for a brother who was a stranger to know me. Later, I reacted by holding secrets deep within my being so they would not be so divulged as easily as reading a book.

"Some months passed, and, in one of the days, I heard a voice again. A familiar voice, laughing, but also sounding far away and lonely. He said, 'Please, just always be my friend!' But the conversation was cut short by an electronic error, and it was as if it had never happened at all! Whether my alien brother will ever share in my life again, I don't know. I can only wait for time to pass and seasons to create a spring again. But no one will be dearer to me than this brother who entered my life and left it richer through many re-discoveries."

Her companion smiled. He told her, "The world is full of people, and it is so frighteningly evident, all the empty shoes waiting to be filled. It is like being in a vast building where there are rows and rows and racks and racks of empty shoes. Then, suddenly, someone stands before us in a pair filled. Out of the millions, someone is there, an alien brother or sister in shoes we recognize. It is hard to fathom this, right? Maybe we could feel comfortable with this idea if we saw it in a fantasy movie. But we think of others with leading roles, not realizing that we ourselves are the performers."

Sport was amazed, and her eyes opened. She saw her companion in full light as she understood that his voice was identical to the one who had said to her, "Please just always be my friend!"

This time, she did not want him to get away so easily. "Sit down," she commanded. "I need to tell you my story!"

# Chapter 2: Patriot's Pass

"It was long ago," she told her friend, now seated for a story. "The world was different then. Well, not so different. But we were just on the beginning border of today's citizen technology."

He raised a questioning brow.

"Well, no internet, for example. No telephones, except in people's houses. We were all disconnected. Sadly, we still are."

She saw that he was anxious to understand her meaning. She began her story:

*Virginia, 1986*

Sport thought with a touch of Scottish determination: *It takes a lot of strong will to tear oneself away from leisure so rarely found.* She was enjoying a chaise lounge view of a weaving sunset. But she jumped up, ready for another marathon. Her friends would have to understand, the fast clocks would have to slow and leave her time to put together the rest of her webbing life. *Things never happen by chance*, she believed. *Everything that happens has meaning, even if it is hidden in the superconscious beyond.* To Sport, Easter vacation had to be a time to take a look at what was happening in the world. Not just her own little world of education, children, and routes in and out of the city. This had to be a learning vacation. So, she grabbed her purse (too scantily filled with essentials) and a small suitcase, and she set out on Good Friday. She realized how exciting it would be to share the coming adventure with someone, but she couldn't think of a single person who would step out of their work week for one day to go along with her.

She felt an urgency to leave early in the morning, and she would later have to claim an emergency for not telling anyone that she would not be there for the workday. It was just a teacher's workday. The children were already away on vacation. Sport thought that there was more important work to be done elsewhere.

In her mind, she searched for the perfect companion for this adventure, and she decided upon one who shared her love for education, vacation and adventure: She recognized her traveling companion in the lovely smile of Christa McAuliffe, the school teacher who had boarded the ill-fated Challenger spacecraft recently.

*So, Christa, our beautiful angel, astronaut and teacher, you are going to be my friend on this Good Friday journey. Hear me, dear Christa: The first time I learned of you, I wanted to call you, write you, race out to you and beg you, "Take me with you!" I wanted your story, the very heart and pulse of blood you poured into teaching, just like me! But on my teacher's salary, I have not had the money nor resources to replicate your intimate steps of home, children and admirers who share your dream and excitement! So, I have for us just a short trip, traveling slowly today in a true American 55 mph. Our lives go so much faster than that. Our ideas and dreams race through time and space. Some hear and some respond. For today, however, you and I are both missing persons!*

Inside her car, Sport checked her watch It was 10:55 a.m. She told Christa that they were being followed by a land-type space cruiser, and that it was okay, because it would pass them by, not knowing how high the two of them would fly.

"We're going to buy that dream for all the kids of the world," she said. "You, Thomas Jefferson and I! We have a frontier to cross. You led the way to it. You jumped in that module, and all we sent was our love. I wished I could have touched you, hugged you, could have taken all those living steps that you walked in history. But I learned that I mustn't hurry this day of journey into fulfilment. I must travel by man's laws while trying to fulfill God's purpose and plan for me. This is a message that you exemplified. Christa, help us today and tomorrow to let go of fear and to fly into knowledge as you did.

"Do you understand that at the end of the day, I walked out of my classroom yesterday? I decided on three things for this quick vacation: my shoes for climbing, author James Metcalf's, *A Teacher's Prayer*, and our beloved American flag. But today, I left all those at home. I wanted complete freedom and the option to mark allegiance to a flag that flies the colors of the world. This is a trip to search our Founding Fathers' heritage. In starting a new nation, they were envisioning a new future for the world. The children of the world now are being lost in their maturing. They look like all other drowning people who have given up their childlike faith and their far-reaching dreams. I guess, Christa, there are a lot of teachers out

26

there like you and me, but they are afraid to take that one step for man and the giant leap for mankind. Maybe, after you and I understand the heritage intended for us all, we can get other teachers ready for an ultimate field trip. Maybe the nation then won't be pounding on the locked doors of the schools, and we will have teachers willing to unlock their creative resources without fear, when they can teach without pressure."

The day was sunny and warm. Sport had the car windows rolled down. She realized that the road was flowing smoothly. She might soon have to turn her car air-conditioner on.

"We're on our way to Monticello, Thomas Jefferson's home on his little mountain, Christa. Today, you and I suffer no gender discrimination. You, so light and lovely, and me: I am a missing nobody today. Whee!"

She was driving 55 mph, and no one cared, except the man who didn't yield his big Eldorado. Sport blew her horn. There was no traffic rush. She saw Chickahominy Creek beside them. She thought of all the Indians who had disappeared from these lands. She turned her attention back to the road and to her traveling companion.

"I hear bells when I'm happy, Christa, and today we are going to ring the bells of schools for freedom, even if it means we have to drive to Philadelphia to touch the Liberty Bell or to walk right up the steps of the White House. These children need education that is as fast-paced as our space-time. God, I should stop talking and watch for the Richmond bypass."

She checked her watch. Eleven twenty-five a.m. Seventy-six miles to Charlottesville, still on the freedom road. She saw the first tiny yellow butterfly. The Richmond bypass to Charlottesville appeared to the right. Sport got goosebumps.

"Christa, do you know that there are sixty-year-old people living right here in Virginia who have never visited Monticello or Charlottesville? It would be awful to imagine all our school children who would never see the contagious magical wonder of Jefferson's home, where dreams were conceived and built."

Sport sighed.

"Hey, world, why are you all asleep? Let's take a break, Christa, I feel like I ate a butterfly! It's 11:35 a.m., and there is the Richmond Times Dispatch in the machine in front of a little restaurant here in Manakin."

27

Sport read an article during lunch about lightning strikes at Cape Canaveral. She told Christa about her theory about what went wrong with Challenger. It was based on an article she had read the previous fall in a magazine. After the disastrous flight, Sport recalled the article.

"Lots of research and studies, Christa, that lightning strikes twice and more. See page 31, National Wildlife Magazine, October/November 1985. Read the article, 'Should we have built Cape Canaveral There?' In Florida, lightning repeatedly strikes bulges in the coastline such as Cape Canaveral. Did storm sea breezes conspire with electrical charges to cause your fall? Oh, Christa, why did it have to happen? And here you are, sitting in this booth with me, and no one has spoken, noticed or cared. We'll just move on. But we have to stay at fifty-five miles per hour, as I am not going to lose my freedom to a traffic summons on Good Friday."

They were fifty-one miles from Charlottesville when Sport looked up to see a bridge pillar upon which had been scribbled "Trust Jesus!" *He must have walked a road to freedom, too,* Sport thought. She told Christa to hang in there with her, that there would be no rest stops. She saw a bus that was branded, "Travel Mates." She pointed to it and told Christa that the name described them and that she had chosen Christa. She turned on the radio and heard music by Neil Diamond and Gordon Lightfoot. She was doing a steady fifty-miles-per-hour when they passed a state police patrol car with aimed radar but no lights aglow. He was a friend, she knew. She remembered that she had left her "Teacher's Prayer" and a collage that she had made for the children of "Jefferson's Ten Rules." These rested beside her disconnected answering machine, so that if anyone went to much trouble to look for her, they could figure out where she had gone.

She had a sudden feeling of hope. She felt it coming from Christa. It made her feel euphoric. She began to blurt things happily.

"Christa, we're in good company, loving our kids. The whole world is going to love their kids more. Oh, we're coming up to Shannon Hill! God, I wonder when I'll get to Ireland? I wished my new car had cruise control. It's hard doing a soft touch on the accelerator when I am feeling so much excitement. I just saw a hawk in flight! It was so pretty! Now these foothills are starting to flow into one another, like a harmony within the land mass. I love sky, space, trees and seas. I told a friend once, 'I don't ask for much in life, just those.' He said, 'Well, they are expensive!' But today, Christa, they are free! And it's Good Friday! Look at these hills and trees. By these very trees, the American Revolution fired its musket balls. Now, without foliage, these trees seem like branching limbs of history, but they are stark, in waiting, in need of remembrance."

She thought she saw amusement on Christa's face. She pointed to a sign that indicated Charlottesville and Scottsville at Exit 24. She took it, but yellow butterflies and absorbed thoughts put her eighteen miles out of the way. *Wow, missing turns or taking a wrong one on mountain roads should teach me to be alert*, she chided herself. She made an apology to Christa.

But then they were on the grounds of Monticello, Jefferson's "little mountain." Sport spoke every feeling and sensation from her soul:

*In these warm and chilled mountain breezes, Monticello is a haven of peace for me today. There's silence instead of the busy networks of technology, except for the slurring of car wheels through the gravel parking area. Just the natural sounds of human voices and footsteps of people willing to broaden their horizons with a visit to a special history. The sun is so bright on the Scotch broom grass beside the parking lot. The seeds had been sown by the Scots as a trail of remembrance.*

*Spring bursts from every vein of the dogwood trees. My body is already hungry again, but my soul needs peace from the pressures of every instant a clock to meet, a bell demanding a response, a parent to call. How I wish I had my children here to share this quiet adventure! Some of them are just electronic vibrations of energy trapped in a ragged life with no escape. They have no choice but to absorb pain after pain until they hit the breaking point and either grab the drugs or pull the rope for an exit. Life for them is a bum deal.*

She knew Christa had been reading her. She said to her, "Yesterday I put myself between two big boys with fists at the ready and just stood there. People thought I had been foolish, but I felt no fear. You see, it offered them a flash of thinking which had never been put to them before. We must teach them to think freely as the wind, liberated from tones of voice and fight-or-flight responses. Many of our kids feel pressured by curriculum, and many find it irrelevant. We need to realize as adults that our children are reaching a higher degree in a shorter period of time than the K-to-12 current system. The technology that launched you into space is launching the present population of kids into the future today, while their educators are climbing out of yesterday. You understood this, Christa, with your friendly wave and interviews. You were teaching about the frontiers of adventure. I try to stoke their creativity and encourage their sensitivity until they reach that acceptable age of someone's work calendar."

The bus from the parking area to Jefferson's home had arrived to take the visitors up the small mountain to the house.

"Folks who have their tickets may board the bus," a man authoritatively declared. The line was forming like the lines for the buses to take the children home from school. As he thundered the declaration repeatedly, Sport thought, *Wow, is this the way kids perceive us at school? A bunch of bombarding messages received only by the ears tuned to the right frequency?*

"There will be more buses. I'm in no hurry," Sport told the lady at the ticket window for Monticello admissions. "Do you have a special rate for teachers playing hooky?" She could hear Christa chuckle behind her.

When they arrived on the spacious grounds where sat Jefferson's home, Sport thought that it did not seem so crowded as people paced around the lawn and gardens. Eventually, ticket holders formed another line to visit the mansion. Monticello as a preservation had its own story to tell, finances always being a concern, and Sport and the visitors soon learned that Thomas Jefferson faced financial strains all his life.

"Christa, as you look around, did you hear that Mr. Jefferson even had to make nails for additional income? Jefferson built his mansion to house his multitudinous interests in humanities and sciences, and his mountaintop sings his dreams in the chilly winds. He did it for us! It is so quiet here in the afternoon breezes today, except for the songs of the birds, and the horizon of the valley is so far away that the earth's curvature is evident. There beyond, Christa, is the sea of space that beckoned you to your journey of forever!"

As she explored the grounds, Sport listened to people talking. Walking the paths, people were still in lines. They were either silent to savor the specialness of where they were, or they were also giving directions to one another, especially to the children. *We certainly have learned how to form lines well,* Sport thought, as all the heads watched their descent down a hill. She risked a glance up to see what they were missing: a fantastic vapor trail in the sky, beautiful like a comet tail, and she thought of Christa.

In the garden, she observed a lone daffodil. She heard a child raise a respectful question about the flowers and the father's reply, "There are times, Tommy, when you are so silly!" And Sport took the child's hand in her mind, and she shouted for him, "Butterflies of spring! I understand! Cocoons for protection and wings for flying! Thank you, God, I'm flying!"

She heard a notebook page lapping in the wind. Someone spoke the truth: "You can see for miles out there. There are the towns in the valley, but I bet it was so wild here when he built his house!"

*Mr. Jefferson, when the Masters set you on your course, did you even know? Did you sense that it was impossible to go back and fit the mold of being another nail? Maybe the nails you made were your creative mirth to be hammered into many grains. Here at Monticello, maybe another view of you shines through.*

Before she ascended the upward return path to the mansion, Sport stopped two college boys and asked, "Is there a path across?" One replied, "No, but you can cut across." There it was, the invitation to dare in his simple answer. Somehow the young man still tapped into the underground reservoir of his mischievous creativity.

She spoke to the gardener beneath the shaded hat. Up turned a glamorous face. She was like a glass vase of violets and tulips, every vein of her life vibrating in the spring breezes like the flowers set on an outdoor table.

Sport whispered to Christa, "When we stop and enjoy what others are doing, we find the strength to continue on. The world glides through its natural orbit, and we could not notice. We miss its natural rhythms in our classrooms, offices and high rises. So much high-tech maneuvering. Look, Christa, they have protected this yellow poplar tree with a lightning rod. Why couldn't we develop lightning rods to protect our spaceships? I'm thinking about our stations in space for the kids of the future. Their safety."

She saw the appreciative love in Christa's face. To make her laugh, Sport shouted out to the sky, "Hello, Mr. Jefferson! You put lightning rods in our Declarations of Independence! You are wonderful!"

A fourteen-year-old passed by wearing a T-shirt that said, "Born in the U.S.A." A black-and-white zebra swallowtail visited the sweet-williams beside them. It felt like truly a wonderful spring.

Sport felt tears welling. She turned to her companion.

"Dearest Christa, please come along another day…this has been our Good Friday!"

# Section 2: Crash and Burn

# Chapter 3: Freedom's Flight

Sport reported to her friend, who was still listening attentively to the story of her weekend quest, that the next morning she awoke to the memory of Christa's leaving.

"But I didn't feel sad!" she told him. "More than anything, it felt like I had witnessed her successful launch! And when I got in the car and turned on the radio, happy music was playing lyrics that caught my ear: 'Some Saturday morning, I'm going away with my friend.'"

She looked at him. "Come, be in the car with me. Imagine it. I will be your eyes."

He understood. He closed his eyes to focus on the imagery that she would create:

"The globe is rimmed in halo pink as the sun climbs its mountainous way. The blue of infinity extends beyond sight, and the giant eye opens. The stark trees somehow relax in their appointed places. Day rise! Sun rise! Hope rise! Another night survived for a resurrection to try again. Happiness fills my morning, and joins the other feelings: wonder, awe and exhilaration. A silent praise escapes me. The sky is filled with geese flying to home in the North. Their flight of magic guides the dawn into the day. Everything around me is both so near and so far. It is another day to chase a dream. Dare and guess. Laugh and escape. This is me today, a child of the universe. My mission is unwritten and seemingly unknown, except by me. I know there is a love that contains truth, the truth that eliminates all counterfeits that create havoc. Somewhere along the way to my spot on this road, I fell off the bridge of anxiety into the water of peace. This is my time to discover, and it has come in freedom's flight."

Her companion opened his eyes, rose from his chair, and took the passenger seat next to Sport.

"The Constitution Trail was made really not by knowledge but by spirit," she told him. The rolling hills stole her breath. Rounding a curve, in a split second popped into view a small white church with St. Frances of Assisi standing outside. Sport felt an intuition to pull over and catch her breath. The view at that spot was magnificent. Just ahead, at a second sharp curve, a tractor trailer going too fast negotiated the curve poorly and hogged both lanes of the two-lane road. Sport and her companion saw that they would have been on that curve had she not slowed to the shoulder in front of the church.

"God!" she exclaimed. She looked at her friend. "The intuitive must be used every day to keep it sharp and to keep it alive."

Sport felt peaceful as she resumed her journey along the Constitution Road. She felt at the right place at the right time. She saw a near-empty parking lot in the little town of Scottsville and turned in and parked. It was the parking lot of a funeral parlor. She had just buried her past, and today she was to begin her life with or without St. George. She chose the lot because it was across the street from a beauty shop. She darted across the street and went in.

The lady in the beauty parlor said that she would do Sport in a little bit.

"I'm not in a hurry," Sport told her. "I'm a Virginian!"

The lady looked at Sport, wearing her purple dress, as if she were from another planet. She proceeded with her customer. Later Sport asked for a straight pin because she had lost her broach. The woman let her reach into her desk, an old teacher's desk. Sport found the pin cushion. In return, she gave the woman her last teacher's card when she was leaving, because she suspected that the woman had once been a teacher.

"Thank you for being here," Sport told her. "I feel at home in Scottsville." In the back, a quiet clock chimed its halfway mark between eleven and noon. She could still hear it as she stepped back out into the daylight of the town. It chimed the peace that she was feeling.

"Love begins with the people you meet," Sport told her friend. "When the spirit flows freely, self is forgotten. In those moments, there is no standard time. Love strengthens according to the non-standard time you give each person. Love pours freely, like these tears."

She said it to explain why she was crying a river long hidden. She didn't need to pretend anything false in front of her companion. The tears were a sweet surrender.

*You've come home to Scottsville to begin living anew,* she thought. *Here, in this town, the birthplace of a nation and freedom extended its roots. In this moment, I feel the reality of being and the heart of knowing. Hello, world! Hello, out there, stars in space!*

A little mocking bird lit on a van across the way. She looked as if she also had flown down Constitution Road to find a homing place. In its stance and song, she sang that she was home and afraid to go away.

*I have nowhere to go, little bird, and no place to be,* Sport thought.

She remembered a church a block away and went there. Inside St. George's Church, she listened to the organ. An organist was practicing. He played the same rhythm of peace that Sport had inside her, a rhythm that oscillated like the outlines of the distant mountain ranges along the horizon. She turned her eyes to a painting that showed St. George as a knight in shining armor. There he was in the Holy Land, slaying the dragon from his unicorn's mount, while the beautiful young princess looked on. Sport had forgotten this painting in the church. She had been yearning for her St. George, and now she knew that she had been yearning only to find this place.

The night before, in the motel, she had been handed a child's sweet gift, and in its pages had been the precious magic unicorn of love. She had read the tale of the unicorn with the ease of choice. But the real world, she realized, held different turns of choices, one after another, and a different time on the turn for each one. The beautiful day twisted and curved through her perception of it and created new segments of adventure. On her current adventure, she did not intend for there to be hide-and-seek games. Her yearning had delivered her to this church and her seat before the knight and the dragon. Obeying her intuitive imaginings brought her to this beauty beyond mountaintops of belief. She never knew that "Climb Every Mountain" in song could be a reality. She didn't know that love could reach so far, ascend so high, and bring such glorious peace.

Her "St. George" and she had only seen each other twice. They had lived eight separate years on separate shores. She had been exhausted from attempting to survive alone. Her mind had always been strong, but her body was weakened from the scarcity of rest, the over-taxing of the soul and the missing of companionship.

Sitting before the painting of the slain dragon, Sport realized that she could not play games with unicorns and dragons. Her body had felt moments of rapture in the little chapel of holy wonder, and it had freed her spirit a spit of time to soar jet trails into space. She whispered softly, "I'll listen for your call again. I know you are here!" The release had been that of her loneliness.

She heard children playing outside.

*Dear St. George, do you hear the beautiful children? For them we must do everything for their survival! For them, you have sent your message. You have proven to me that love and telepathy are stronger than any arms race. Let's give presents of gifted education for everyone! The first gift is the understanding of the delicacy of the human satellite of brain. Six ounces of love generation for the saving of the whole human race. Arms race, goodbye! Education, hello!*

Her companion had slipped into the church and had quietly taken a place beside her. He had heard her thoughts, and he looked at her questioningly, a request for her to explain more.

"I see one God who is outside the speck of earth's time," she began. "He is weightless. When we yearn for Him and take the leap into space and acclimate to weightlessness, then the mind can soar. Imagine that we are not the only ones in the seeking, that there are intelligences out there who may yet try to contact us. We exist in an expanding universe that demands our reaching to stay connected.

"Easter can be every day as the world awakens to the rising truth that our measures of intelligence are useless. Intelligence is organic, responsive; it grows beyond the six ounces. We must throw out the limiting assumptions that we can teach only 'x' number of gifted children because there are only 'y' number of spaces and 'z' amount of money. All have unmeasurable potential. But what we do is to sentence our kids to 181 days of school, fastening them in seatbelts of small-scale desks that cramp and bind. We give them schedules of stand, sit, bend and read. The books on their backs sometimes weigh more than the children. The weight makes them round-shouldered and old. Let the adults who haven't carried books for a while help. How about a grandparent or two for every kid in the world? That wouldn't require tax dollars. All it would take is people who love one another to communicate and be willing to pioneer a new history of enlightenment."

Their conversation continued in the car. Sport felt like turning on the windshield wipers to clean off the bug-stained windows so she could enjoy the view. She flashed her lights at a sage green government car to stop its head-on race toward her. When the driver saw her face, he looked surprised. He had been preoccupied while in his hurry. Sport's feeling of being startled didn't arrive until the car disappeared quickly from the view of her mirror. The fragility of life was her realization, and this created a feeling of urgency to get things done before time ran out.

*On the Constitution Road, I found my hero in the little chapel of St. George of the Masses,* she thought when she had recovered herself. She wanted to join in the flight of the unicorn with her Saint George to check on the well-being of the children of the world. She imagined a prayer chain that began in that church for the children. Its purpose would be to fulfill her wishes that all of them would run freely, laugh loudly and clap their hands in international joy.

She told her travel companion, "Children can learn that love opens doors, cleans the skies and allows the trees to grow forever."

He threw her a questioning look.

"The lives of our trees are sawed short," she explained. "Their historical length of stay on our planet doesn't reach its potential. Our children have the sensitivity to care about something like this. It is respect for life. We should take the munitions from the hands of the kids across the world, model respect for them, and teach them responsibility and love. Kids relate to animals and plants like trees. Teaching a child to put a tree in the ground for each one sawed off in its historical life is a great way to teach and model respect for life. I will never forget my feelings as a young girl when I found a landmark tree over 350 years old that had been chopped like a sentinel that had lost its head. It was on an Easter weekend like this one. My neighbor, seeing that I was upset, suggested that I plant another one for the next couple thousand years of freedom."

Her companion smiled slightly and nodded.

They were heading home. Sport finished the holiday feeling electrified by awe. She had cried because of the beauty of truth. She had seen that the power of love is what energizes the possibilities of dreams coming true. She had noticed, for the first time, that the trust of youth was the greatest national resource. And she had seen and heard her own purpose through the friendship with Christa. Sport had seen that remarkable woman laugh on the day that the rest of the world cried.

# Chapter 4: The Power of Words

Days later, Sport had just finished her first freelance article that she intended for a psychology magazine, and, with nervous feelings, she had raced down the freeway to seek a friend's counsel. She wanted his bright opinion before she asked for an opportunity to moonlight as a newspaper columnist. She walked into the brightly lit new office building with the sunlight streaming in, a cheerful visitor from outer space. At least, that is what she felt like on this red-headed day. She was invited to take a seat. Sport recognized that she needed a shampoo and set, but the importance of this visit superseded that. After all, this friend had seen her from elegant to ordinary. Today wasn't ordinary, but her new purple dress and high heels would have to suffice.

The trim and stylish secretary looked like a matinee idol's choice. She was lovely. But Sport would not feel daunted in her hope for success by dwelling on her comparison. She sat there, holding her excellent copy. In a while, her friend appeared, and Sport's "Good morning, Mr....." was cut off by his abrupt mentioning that he was busy, but that he would make some moments with her shortly. That reluctant courtesy set the tone for the morning.

While she waited again in the lobby, a disenchanting pedestrian came through the front door. He immediately engaged the secretary in busy advertisement conversation. He asked her how they wished to have their new advertising poster framed for the wall. What color frames would look best?

He cast an eye toward Sport, winked and said, "Did you know that this week people are wearing the colors that define them?" Looking back at the secretary, he said, "I see the frames in here being perfect in red and green on your white wall. But I might be partial, because I am Italian!" Sport spoke up and suggested that green and yellow would be very attractive.

One of the massive mahogany double doors to the lobby opened, and Sport's friend motioned for her to enter. Sport took a seat at the corner of his desk where she could see both the activities outside through the wall of glass behind him and the side of his face as he read her manuscript. She was surprised by his frowning. His eyes were piercing the document like a legal razor, or maybe "laser" was a better term.

His eyes snapped in her direction, and he asked, "Is this privileged information, yes or no?"

Sport was caught off guard. His tone felt like attack. She answered, "Yes," concluding that this would end the conversation.

But he nodded at the document. "You're made of tough stuff," he told her.

That was unexpected. Sport could only remember one other time when he had paid her a compliment, and she had clung to that thread for years whenever she went through seasons of self-doubt.

He handed the document back to Sport. "You're the brightest woman I have ever met."

*What?* Sport didn't believe this blarney, but she saw that the General (as she thought of him) recognized that she had some value to the human race.

She walked to the door, turned and looked him squarely in the eye and said, "That doesn't sound like you."

"The facts are what we are interested in," he replied. "You're a good writer. You're a better teacher. You should think about whom you really want to help. You are someone special to your students." Then he put himself back to his own occupations.

"Thank you," Sport answered, but she didn't feel like any special person in anyone's world. She walked resolutely to the front door, not pausing to smile at the beautiful secretary.

She remembered having seen a large bird's nest in a tree in her yard early that morning. All she could think was, *The nest is empty! There is no one there, and neither is there someone for me at home.* She clutched her article to her chest. She sighed. *It's just me and my writing in this great big world. Alone. Seeking a place to belong.*

She started her car and threaded through the side streets to the freeway. She really needed to go to the bank to get cash, but she was tired and just wanted to leave the city. She had returned from her weekend to Scottsville on Easter Sunday to rest because in her very seams of existence she felt totally fatigued. But the thought of the downstairs apartment blaring high amplifier noise from its ceiling to her floor ruined the notion of returning home. She drove silently, relishing the restorative quiet in her automobile.

The General had unsettled her. She felt foolish and ashamed and didn't know why.

And then she did.

*The dream-memories are driving me crazy!*

With every year that passed, Sport's dreams gained stickiness and strength. She smelled the steamy, tropical aroma of countryside that she had never visited. She felt the rough, three-dimensional bark of the trees. She touched the beautiful light-bronze skin of people who caressed her face with their hands. She met real people whom she had created in her imagination during the day. Always, those were the ones whom she had given names. When she awoke, all these faded as vestiges of dreams. But, years later, she recalled people and places as if they came from memories and not dreams. The line between her imaginary creations of the day and the fantastical dreams of the night was washing out in the high tides of her fantasies.

One recent day, Sport thought: *I think I am running two streams of memories.* That night, she dreamed about a sailing ship bringing relatives from Scotland to America. It tossed horribly about in the sea of an Atlantic storm and awakened her. She was as thirsty as if she had been drinking salt water. In the bathroom, she emptied her mug containing her toothpaste and toothbrush and filled it with tap water. She drank two full cups. She turned on soft music to lull her back to sleep. She drifted to a planet busy with life in silo cities arising from fields of edible flowers. She was happily working in the field and chatting with a friend when a shadow plunged the area into darkness, and a giant sucking sound accompanied the emptying of breathing. Sport sat up in the bed in a panic. She couldn't breathe. She still heard voices screaming from inside the dream left behind, "Run to the caves! Breathe!" Sport fled quickly and blindly through her apartment and found herself gasping in the chilly night air. She was startled to find herself outside in that condition, but shocked more by an impression in the back of her mind:

*We left the planet!*

But the next morning, the nervous feelings produced by the dreams dissipated in the glorious sunshine of a day that went well. Only once in all her occupations did Sport pause and think to herself, *Did I dream about a planet that had to be abandoned?* She tried, but she could not recapture the details.

Still, days came and went, and Sport in silent moments began to struggle with the distinctions of dreams, memories and her own imaginative creations. The distraction pushed her time limits. Lesson planning time and time for the children gave up some territory to an activity that came from a strong intuition that motivated Sport: She began to write about what was happening to her. The writing became the only possible thing that could distract Sport from her children.

One night, she sat upright in bed from a sleep disturbed by a feeling that someone was present. In the moonlight on her window sill sat an angel. He didn't have wings, but Sport knew that he was an angel because everything about his demeanor and his glow in the moonlight proclaimed it.

"You want to know everything," he told Sport. "But you are not ready. Your memory is unreliable. The world is about to change quickly for the worst. You haven't experienced what you need to know to help the next generation. You must travel through this time, feel the pain of people and die to them. You must forget everything that came before. You have to be like them. Be brave. Take the journey now. There is not much time left."

He disappeared. Sport sat up in bed. She realized that when she had just sat up in the bed, she had been dreaming. She rubbed her arms to be certain that now she was fully awake.

*I will forget what the angel said to me*, Sport told herself with dismay. *I have to write it down!*

She dashed to her computer and typed a document. First, she wrote the angel's message and the pieces she could remember of the dream that presaged him. Then she spent the next hours writing the article that she would let the general see. It told of her parallel memory streams, her creative imaginings and her dreams.

Now, driving home from her encounter with the General, she heard again his words: "You're a good writer. You're a better teacher. You should think about whom you want to help."

"I don't know!" Sport screamed aloud in the car. But she did know what the angel told her.

She had to take the journey now.

She decided to spend a few days in a pretty area of the state about an hour north of her home town. It was Tuesday evening, and she had a few vacation days left from work. She had only to stop at her apartment to get some things like cosmetics, shoes and clothes.

# Chapter 5: Flight by Night

*Hello to freedom!* Sport descended the long brick stair steps to the winding driveway. The cool moist air of the evening invigorated her skin. She opened her car door and put everything inside quietly so as not to awaken the sleeping neighbors. She pressed the key into the ignition of her new car and felt the exhilaration of adventure charging through her veins and brain to set off an atomic bomb of joy. The rush of her feelings carried her to the turn-around of the cul-de-sac and up the hill. Then she remembered to turn on the car lights, as the bright street lights had been sufficient lighting before. But wisps of fog from the evening moisture on the windshield put amber halos around the street lights. She turned on her radio and settled into driving through the still early morning hours, maybe until two. She found her way to the freeway, not from habit, but from having read road signs all her life and depending upon them to be in the right place at the right time.

She crossed the final span of a series of bridges that passed over terrain where colonists had once braved chilling winters and found potent enemies in the disease-carrying mosquitos of summer. She wondered what other unexpected warriors of the virgin forests they had to encounter. Sport had a habit of musing historically, but she remembered to be intent in her drive through the moonlit night while there was hardly anyone else on the road except truckers. She zipped the speedometer dial up to make flying miles through the night.

She noticed ahead flickering amber lights of a big rig pulled over to the shoulder. To her, the lights tapped the message, "There is caution to be heeded! Careful!" Then suddenly in the headlight's beam was the large carcass of an animal that had been mauled by the night wheels of a speeding car or truck. *Had the radios of truckers alerted the one near her to the impending obstruction in the road,* she wondered?

Sport decided to keep her eyes keener in alertness. She put down her window for fresh air to help alleviate a new wave of sleepiness. She had had little sleep in the past several days. In the opposite lanes, another trucker had pulled over to the side, perhaps to bed for the night or just to take a pause from long driving. She suddenly realized that her flying pass in the night just might be observed by these road veterans of the highways. Nearing an unfamiliar intersection, she slowed to read all the signs, but another truck pulled over there slowed her even more. There it was, the very intersection she was hunting! It seemed as if the truckers were pointing the way to her Charlottesville destination on this first morning of her vacation adventure.

Making her turn, Sport breathed a sigh of relief that she had not made a wrong choice earlier that would put her going in the direction of Richmond. Shortly in the road, she came upon the demise of another animal, and she swerved and avoided a direct hit. The drive was beginning to feel like a demolition derby. Fortunately, the animal had not been a skunk, but she had not had time to grasp the true proportions of the creature. She focused her eyes on the moonlight silhouetting the trees along the highway and glanced at the multitudinous stars. The night sky calmed her and gave her feelings of peace and release.

*I need this, just time to feel the wonderful freedom of not following overwhelming schedules and not having a place to be. I just want my few days of quiet and rest.*

Already she had forgotten what the angel told her.

But she thought of her adventure as a venture along the highway of intuition and that she would be making choices at its intersections that would direct her to the mountaintops of cresting wonder. The gas gauge was still in good position, so she wouldn't need to purchase gasoline until morning. She pulled a piece of a cracker from her purse and began to nibble it. She had heard a radio broadcast once that described how people survived long periods of time on just small crumbs of food. She had taught the children in her classes to nibble and to chew each bite thirty times to experience the best flavor. So, in the car, she began her experiment in rationing little bits of goodies.

*If only I had brought water along,* she mused. *Water shouldn't be so hard to get, but, then again, I am on a deserted span of freeway in the middle of the night. There are no towns for miles around.*

She was grateful for her intuition to lease a car back in February so that she would have a reliable car for taking a trip over Easter vacation. She snuggled deeper into her seat and turned on the heater as the night began to close tightly around her body. The mileposts flying behind seemed to be in tune to the rhythms of the music playing in the car. The wavelengths of time carried her back to Constitution Road by the morning hour of five o'clock. The long night was catching up with her. She daydreamed that she saw patriots laden with heavy packets on their backs marching towards the rolling mountains.

*A time-slip into the past,* Sport mused. *Wonder, enchantment and awe that our nation broke the hold of monarchy only to teeter on the edge of new democracy!*

She shook her head to dispel the sleepiness and the marching figures disappeared. The mountain road looked like two ribbons cutting through the darkness, lit by her headlights. The road had no street lights, only an occasional mailbox without numbers.

But the beginning of this journey was one recently made and familiar even in the night. Sport felt the dryness of her throat like parchment with rough edges. She hoped when she arrived again at the beautiful little church named St. George of the Masses that it would have a light and that the priest's small home overlooking the mountain meadow would be welcoming the anticipated dawn. She turned a corner into a dirt driveway, moved up the rising slope and stopped her car. Taking her keys in hand, she wearily got out of the car. She walked toward the light on the outside of the parish house, and then she saw to her horror the sad condition of the cross on the side of the church. It was draped in dirty rags, and at its base were two baskets of dead flowers. Lent and Easter Sunday had passed unattended.

*Oh God, what a mockery!* she thought.

She had a moment of feeling dreams crushed in the darkness and the vanquishing of peace. She didn't know where to go. Her instinct told her to go to the town, Scottsville, where days earlier a woman had said to her, "We hope you come back here and settle among us!" It was the pastoral little town of her childhood, a snug hamlet in the Jeffersonian hills. She returned to her car and headed towards the town. Passing through a crossroads made her wonder how many crossroads of decisions she had come to in her life.

Her memory produced the image of a beautiful school building in the hills. *People spend money on their children*, Sport mused. She threaded her way there and parked in front of a dark school bus that apparently was still on Easter vacation.

As her car got cold in the pre-dawn chill, she reached into her overnight case and pulled out her black terry-cloth robe with a white hood and put it on over her clothes. She curled up small for warmth, awaiting the advancing sunrise. When a rooster crowed once and then a second time, Sport shuddered. She felt like she was in her own Garden of Gethsemane. The haze of the dawn, the silence, the almost empty gas tank, the surrealism of the night trip and her thirst made her feel that she was half-awake in a nightmare.

*I just wanted to pursue my dreams and follow my intuition to go on holiday,* she lamented, *so how did I snare this soul-piercing ache in my heart?*

The cold sunrise did not provide additional warmth, but she did not dare to turn on the car engine and use the little remaining gas that would have to be carefully rationed until she could get more. She would wait until the little café she knew in town would be open, where she could get breakfast. And that would have to be a meager breakfast until she could finally get to a bank later in the morning. The banks on that morning would open at ten. She only had five dollars in cash.

She drove into the town at 7 a.m., and hers was the only automobile moving. The street was nearly deserted, so there were plenty of parking spaces. There would be no need to park in the funeral parlor lot. Everything was still closed. Needing water, she thought of another church where she might find some, but when she arrived there, the doors were locked. Nowhere in town was a curbside drinking fountain. She saw in the window of the local department store life-sized rabbit manikins dressed in old-fashioned clothes and wire-rimmed glasses. They peered at Sport like they were frozen in some moment of a stage show that had closed. The early morning town suddenly felt creepy and unfriendly. She knew that this was illusion and that, in reality, the town was just an ordinary, existing town not tuned into her moods.

Sport decided to find a cheerful home where the owners might welcome her and gladly provide a glass of water for the early-morning traveler. She envisioned a house like the ones in bed-and-breakfast brochures. A small way out of town, she pulled into a lovely, inviting driveway flanked with spring flowers. A couple of short curves through the trees finally yielded the view of the house that she had anticipated. But when she got out and approached it, a couple of sleeping dogs tied to posts awakened angrily and strained their leashes as they lunged and growled threats of attack.

She was still wearing her terry-cloth robe. She hadn't put on her coat, which was in the car trunk, because the black leather might make a forbidding appearance for a sunrise, surprise visitor to a home in the country. She thought that the robe was a softer look. She knocked on the front porch door that had glass side windows with white curtains. There was silence, but after a couple of repeated knocks, a small elderly lady came and looked out at Sport.

Sport smiled and called to her, "Good morning! Could I trouble you for a drink of water?"

Her voice excited the dogs to a new crescendo of barking, and the woman with an impassive expression just stared. In a few moments, she disappeared and then re-appeared, this time with an old, frail-looking man. They both refused to answer the door, even with Sport's smile and simple request for water. So Sport swallowed hard, made her way past the manic dogs to her car, turned it around and drove away.

*It's better to leave the dust of this house behind me,* she thought.

Next, she chose a pecan-tree-lined lane, but her hopes diminished as she saw that rusty old cars from different eras were her only greeters along the way. In fact, the drive way led to an unoccupied mansion very run-down from years of weathering without attention. She shuddered from the feeling produced in her by the windows without curtains, the doorways without keys, the steps without greeting, and the lawn without mowing. It was a mansion without love.

Far down the road was a lovely winding lane that crossed through a meadow, overpassed a little stream and climbed a hill to an estate that would be a joy to own. Sport found it such a beautiful sight that the half-mile drive had been worth the suspense of what she would find. The buildings were painted a crisp white, and the fences wound a long line of white-washed wood around the property. Sport thought of milk and her thirst. The lawn was manicured, but there were no cars and no sign of people. She knocked on the door and heard its echoes in the silent house.

*Is there no one in this community except the little old man and little old woman,* Sport wondered?

She felt exhausted. She looked at her gas gauge and decided that exploring was not the answer to her needs. She drove the eighteen miles over the curves and bends of the mountain road that returned her to town and the downtown section. She found an open gas station and filled her tank. She gave the attendant her credit card and asked to use the phone. She dialed a number in a far-off place and had to leave a message on an answering machine. When Sport was finished, she turned and saw a young man in an Air Force uniform. She asked him how to get back to the freeway.

She stopped on the way to town at a McDonald's drive-through for a coffee and egg biscuit. Her cash had now diminished to three dollars. *The banks would surely be open by 10 a.m. even in this little hamlet,* she thought. She remembered a small college campus nearby and thought that she would have time to stop and inquire if they had guest quarters. *It would be nice to spend a couple of days there and do some writing*, she considered.

So, Sport put the car back in motion and flew another piece of the morning up another mountain. She found a detour but didn't fret. She knew the roads from a far memory of days when she used to come to this valley to enjoy its beauty and quiet. It was disquieting now to realize that people in this area were just as cautious of strangers as anyone in the cities. They were afraid even to open doors to a woman requesting a glass of water.

As ten o'clock neared, Sport found the college campus and the front steps of a dormitory where several students were hanging out. She asked them who was the current college President and if a certain old friend was still a professor? Sure enough, both still had those positions there. She headed towards the direction of the President's office. She thought about her purple dress that never showed wrinkles and the high-heeled shoes that she was wearing. All things considered, she didn't think that she looked too bad for the wear of no night's sleep.

She regained the confidence of the President and his memories of her when she laid out her two diplomas on his desk to prove that she was who she said she was. The years had added weight to his person, and she knew that she did not look the same. Bringing the diplomas now proved helpful. It had been part of the exercise of picking the most important things for her vacation and packing them. She had found in this exercise of mental and physical choices that material things often had less value than the dollars that they represented. Her diplomas were something she cherished because of the memories, the work and their personal significance. Some people valued jewelry, but Sport valued her diplomas.

The guest house was open to Sport. She was also invited to lunch with the President's wife, but she declined that offer because she was very tired and just wanted to sleep. The President told her that she could stay just one night because the quarters had already been promised to someone coming in for the big Founder's Day weekend on campus. They would be arriving the following morning.

The red carpet of the guest home elegantly floored the colonial furniture in the best protocol of campus hospitality. The white kitchen reminded her of the fences that she had recently left behind. The refrigerator was empty, but she had the table and telephone that would serve her. She walked into the bedroom, pulled down the bed covers, took off her traveling clothes and fell into bed. Her nap was short and deep. When she got up, she decided to make some phone calls.

*I really should let someone know where I am,* she thought.

And the first person she called was her lawyer!

"I should have a will," she told him. "I am traveling alone, and I should have taken care of this a long time ago." She gave him instructions to prepare one. She had valuable manuscripts and paintings and videos that might be of historical significance. She instructed her lawyer that those should go to a certain children's foundation that had been set up for the education of gifted children. She had devoted her life's work to the education of children and the encouragement of gifted curricula. It had been the way that she had reached out to give in the world. She had given her own children everything that she had, especially measured in time, love and education. The phone call made her weary, but she was determined that her vacation, despite its riskiness, would be worth the taking. Sitting on the side of her bed, she realized that her trip had a subconscious effect of making her feel very mortal.

Her next call was to schedule a haircut and coloring at a beauty salon. In an hour, Sport was out the door and ready to bring a zingy, youthful look to her new adventure. The charming lady in the salon knew the cuts and colors that Sport described to perfection, plus she had studied four years at a university. This gave Sport confidence in her terrific new look. Transformed from shoulder-length to wind-blown short, her new ash-blonde hair revitalized her appearance. Therefore, Sport decided that the next step would be to find a pair of discount blue jeans and a purple blouse. Driving through the little Wednesday town, she observed that there were no children playing nor pedestrians on the streets. Everything seemed strangely silent.

*Is everyone off somewhere, waiting for something?* Sport wondered.

Heading to a neighboring village shopping center, she noticed that in the countryside the fields weren't ready for spring planting. The ploughing hadn't been done, and the farmers weren't in the fields.

*What's going on here? This is a rural community that always in the past was full of hustle and bustle.* Suddenly she remembered an editorial cartoon that she had seen in a local newspaper. At the time, it had made no sense to her. It illustrated strange looking guns poised for fire, and the caption read, "CRACK!" She thought: *There might be no correlation, but…are the farmers being edged from the land around here?* She wondered about her thought. It felt like an intuition.

Sport found a big discount store anchoring a corner spot in a strip shopping center. Entering the store, she first asked the clerk if she could make credit card purchases.

"Oh, yes, no problem," came the cheerful response.

*Then this is a good affirmation*, thought Sport. *I'm going to buy a pair of jeans for the first time in my life! How crazy is that? But Dad always told me as I was growing up that a girl wearing jeans was committing a sin. I don't know, maybe he would change his mind if he were here during this generation. But I am doing it!*

She found a light blue pair that looked great with a purple blouse that had a big collar and rolled-up sleeves. Then she examined tennis shoes of all brands on countless racks. The real challenge was to find a size that fit her tiny feet. There was no one to help her. It was definitely a self-serve store. But she found a pair that she liked. Gathering her new clothes, she found the clerk and asked, "If these things fit, can I wear them? My wool dress is so hot!"

Observing her blue wool dress, the clerk agreed, "Oh, yes! You can remove the tags and bring them to the register. You're dressed much too warmly for seventy-degree weather."

Sport emerged from the dressing room feeling like a new butterfly. The clerk removed the labels that Sport had missed and escorted her to the checkout counter. Sport watched as the clerk slid the card through the machine, and, moments later, numbers of approval came flying to its tiny grey screen. Sport focused on the numbers with interest and memorized them.

*These might be fun for my "Master Mind" game,* she laughed to herself. *I'll compare them against the license plate numbers I see on the road.* She had made up a game of number association to entertain her during long hours of driving. As the clerk put her wool dress in a bag, Sport thought: *Well, here's some food for thought. Maybe I'm not traveling by myself after all! Maybe there is some mystery person behind a computer giving me clues in numbers and strange observations in a game, like Chance cards in Monopoly...go ahead, win, stop, lose, go directly to jail, heaven or hell!*

She was about to smile at her thoughts, when she looked around the store and noticed what seemed like hundreds of sale signs on all the aisles and racks. Some said, "Gigantic Fire Sale! Everything Must Go!" Yet there were few people in the store and even fewer buying. Glancing outside, Sport saw that the parking lot showed little semblance of activity.

It depressed her mood a little.

*What is happening around here?*

Suddenly, she remembered her lack of cash, and she became concerned about the time. She glanced at her watch. *God, it's almost three o'clock! The banks will be closing if I don't pay attention.*

Apprehension began to squeeze her throat. She had been so busy that she had forgotten to have lunch. That seemed less important before. She hurried to her car and began to backtrack to the college campus eleven miles to the south. In several driveways along the way, there were cars parked with their lights on. They seemed like sentinels in the afternoon sun.

*Why?* she wondered. *Okay, maybe they're signaling that there are police cars in the area.* It was another intuitive thought, and a strange one, she realized, because most people simply flash their headlights to do this. But, sure enough, in a little bit she saw two police cars. And something else appeared odd: Some people were driving with windshield wipers beating dry glass. A tractor pulling a cart of hay was zipping at top speed as if there were an impending storm. Sport leaned forward to observe more of the sky through her windshield.

*They do have sudden rain squalls in this area, but I'm just seeing a beautiful blue sky*, she thought. She tried to relax. *Maybe I'm just reading too much into this. But there could be some message for me in these observations.*

The college campus appeared deserted when she arrived. *I guess the big Founder's Day meeting convened early,* she mused. She parked the car and hurried to the guest house. In the hall were gardening tools and cleaning fluids that she did not remember seeing earlier. But then she had been tired, and she felt tired again.

Turning on the television in the living room, Sport found herself confronting too many channels to choose. She rarely had time for television in her life, anyway. Flicking through, she landed on cartoon shows that seemed to have more grown-up messages than pint-sized children would comprehend. And the background music seemed to be in tune with the feelings she had that this area of her childhood was in deep trouble. It was mood music for her mood.

Sport suddenly felt dizzy. She hadn't eaten since that morning, and she realized that she had no food in the guest house. She decided that the best thing would be to go next door and request a cup of coffee. This didn't feel entirely comfortable to do, because she was a person unused to asking anyone for anything. Her normal place was on the giving end.

*Well, being humble is a good exercise*, she told herself. *Not so difficult.*

A little woman with dark hair clipped short answered the door, and Sport introduced herself. The lady turned out to be a professor and invited Sport inside. Her graciousness over coffee opened the flood gates of Sport's emotions. To the woman's wide-eyed amazement, she poured out her story of the past several days and the strange situations in which she had found herself. She asked the woman if she might borrow her bible.

"It has been a long time since I was a bible student, and I would like to read Revelations," she explained.

The woman seemed embarrassed. "I don't have a bible here," she admitted "I keep it locked up in my office at the college."

That seemed strange to Sport. She wondered again what had happened to her little town of long ago. Everyone had a bible in the home.

But the lovely professor had to get ready for a concert. When Sport excused herself to leave, the woman endowed her with bagels, cookies and instant coffee. Sport felt indebted to this lovely and warm human being.

She returned to her quarters and locked the door. In the barren kitchen, she sat down to her feast. But then she considered her circumstances and decided that she should not eat all of it but should save some for later.

She went to re-pack her suitcase. She chose a couple of unneeded items to leave behind, to give her an excuse to return to the campus in the near future.

*I would like to think about living here sometime,* she thought, despite the fact that her intuition told her there were severe problems in the area. But no one was expressing those concerns to her directly.

She needed toothpaste. She checked the time: six-thirty. She hurried to her car. Dusk was deepening, and the air felt cool now. The streets were nearly deserted again.

*A college town with no people.*

It was not the spring vacation that she had envisioned. Upon entering the little corner grocery and pharmacy, she discovered to her surprise that the prices were exorbitant. A tiny tube of toothpaste was five times what she expected to pay. Had this always been the case? She couldn't remember.

As the evening set in, Sport felt something unsettling in the nerve fibers of her soul. It made her think that there was impending danger. About quarter to eight, she decided that staying would not feel restful to her. So, she put the key in a cup in front of the friendly professor's door and quietly left. Needing gasoline, she drove to the little town where she had shopped earlier in the afternoon. She asked the station attendant if there were a water fountain available, and he replied with an annoyed, "No!"

*Thirsty again and with no water, geez,* Sport thought, equally annoyed.

She filled her tank and went in to pay with her treasured credit card. She realized that she still did not have cash. The man ran the card through the terminal while Sport watched the electronic

53

readout. The mastermind of numbers was spelling out a message to her: *Leave!* When the attendant asked if she would like him to clean her windshield, Sport put on a smile and declined, but she added, "Thanks a lot, though!"

She drove to the interstate and headed north. It was jammed with eighteen-wheelers jockeying for position with one another, while the cars, packed to the hilt with people and articles, made occasional dashes in between the trucks in attempts to break free. To Sport it looked like many people were in a northerly caravan, having closed doors to the lives behind them. She wondered why. She considered that she was on the road in search of rest and vacation and that her car was relatively empty.

*Mine is a temporary flight. I travel light,* she thought. She didn't even smile at her own rhyme, because, inside, she felt disquieted by lack of connection.

*Is it my lack of connection or that of people I meet?* she wondered.

She was on the interstate, her life was in motion once again, and Sport willed herself the hope of a better time ahead. But something ominous awaited her just up the road.

# Chapter 6: Interstates

The interstate at night was a flowing ribbon of vehicle lights with a view of a parallel stream moving in the opposite direction. Sport liked the feeling of being back in her car and behind the wheel. She felt in control of her situation again. She had always loved cars. Nothing felt more comfortable to her than her foot on the accelerator, her hands on the steering wheel, and her face smacked by the fresh night air blown in by the fan. Not to mention how she enjoyed the music spinning through the night!

She had tagged along with a furniture truck several miles. It felt like a friend, so Sport decided to follow it. She was certain that the driver must have a citizen's band radio. This made her feel safe. She set her foot on the gas pedal to match his speed and rhythm. After a while, Sport could tell that the driver of the truck realized that he had a guest partner for the evening. She saw his courtesy in flashing lights to signal a passing vehicle that it was safe to come in his lane ahead of him. After a while, he let a new truck take the lead, and somehow Sport found herself driving between them. But it felt like a safe space between competent drivers, and they rolled along, not watching the speedometer or odometer. It was sheer freedom!

Later, traffic became more congested, and impatient drivers took to cutting sharply in front of Sport or running up close behind her. Sometimes she got caught between two cars and another beside her moving at the same rate of speed, so that she was hemmed in. It made her apprehensive, and she maneuvered out of those tight ranges.

*I'm doing some fancy driving*, she admitted to herself. *I might have been a race car driver in some other life.*

Her truck driver companion pulled off at a truck stop, and the night moved along. At some point, Sport noticed that a car following her had been keeping the same distance behind, even when she varied her speed. This made her uneasy enough to pay attention to her surroundings, and she decided to play her number game with the license plates of passing cars. She coded the numbers to letters in her mind. They seemed to spell messages to remind her that she was short of cash and that she should take an exit soon. She often felt as if she were in a game with players unknown, and she wanted to be the one who outwitted them all. Sometimes the messages were strange and frightening, but she trusted her intuition. She felt like she was communicating with beings who looked out for her safety.

Suddenly, when she glanced up towards the sky, she was surprised to see two objects flying in front of her. Their forms were impossible to make out, but from the sound, she deduced that they were helicopters. They were flying low and relatively slowly. Each had triangles in the rear brightly lit in orange. They reminded her of a recent conversation she had had with associates about the meanings of different symbols. One triangle in a book had three words on each side forming the slogan, "Model Courage and Leadership." She was suddenly feeling quite tired as she recalled this illustration, so she decided to begin the process of finding a place to stay for the night.

She discarded the ideas of taking any exits that were not brightly lit. The third one showed a cluster of lights in the distance and signs for a fashionable lodging. Sport parked the car close to the motel office door and went in to register. Seeing a sign that said food service could be had until eleven, she casually remarked to the young man taking her registration that she was very hungry.

"I'm sorry, but our service is closed," he replied. "But there is a restaurant next door that takes credit cards."

She thought it strange that the advertised service would be closed, but she didn't say anything. She was relieved that she could eat on a credit card. Stashing her gold room key in her bag, she trudged back outside to her car and went to the nearby restaurant. As Sport walked in, she noticed two men in business suits who were seated at a table that she had to pass. She sat at a diagonal from them, and one of the men kept eyeing her. She ignored him while studying the menu and enjoying a wonderfully hot coffee that felt like a luxury for her psyche and body after such a stressful day.

The waitress brought Sport a napkin that had a decorative section of red squares. She twirled it absently, but then the geometric pattern caught her attention, and she counted the little red squares. It might have been because she was tired, but the pattern seemed to imprint on her brain, and when she glanced at the wall, she noticed that it also had a white background with red squares.

*It's a diner look*, she told herself, but when she looked at the dull blue carpet on the floor, she found it patterned with grey squares.

*Blue and grey. Of course, like the Civil War*, thought Sport. This made her think of her Social Studies textbook which she used in her teaching. Blue and grey. *I'm in the South, and it is still covered in blue and grey. God, I must be tired! Or is this reality? While I am busy teaching from textbooks, what really is happening in the world is still the same: the blue and grey live on.*

She shook her head to clear her brain, just as the waitress began to serve her food. She sighed to herself.

*Maybe getting out and seeing what is going on in the world is the best education I can possibly have. But it's going to be hard to go back and explain to people what kind of strangeness is engulfing me on this vacation!*

Her appetite soon found the mashed potatoes, roast beef and gravy too fragile under the bombardment of the colors and geometric symbols. She was becoming distracted. Another man entered and began watching her. Another got up to use a payphone in view on the wall. Sport suddenly just wanted to leave. She went to the restroom. When she came out, the waitress carefully took her card and got the approval number. Sport had seen the check number at the top of her bill, and when her mind put it together with the approval number, she felt like she had a message that said, "Get ready, my friend!"

Sport began to leave, but the waitress touched her hand and asked, "Did I give you your card?" Sport verified that it was in her wallet, and then she told the young lady, "Thank you so very much!" as she walked out the door.

But the men at the diagonal table had come behind her to pay their bill, so Sport hurried to her car. Next to it, parked entirely too close, was a green sedan with three dark-haired men sitting in it silently.

*Why are they there?*

Sport was spooked. She quickly backed out of her parking space and bolted through a stop sign at the exit of the parking lot. Instead of going to her paid motel room, she hurried to the interstate. She saw in the rearview mirror that the car that had been parked next to hers had also pulled out, and it was now following her. Sport hit the accelerator and sped into the night. Fearful, she began to think whether there would be other ways in which she could travel. When she saw the lights of a truck stop ahead at the next exit, she had an idea. So, she turned suddenly at the exit at the very last moment in which she could have made the turn. The car behind her continued on.

*Ha!* Sport thought. But she was still anxious. She saw a gasoline attendant and drove up to her.

"Good evening," Sport said. "Do you know if there is a truck going west? I know this sounds strange, but I am writing a book about truck-driver life, and I interview drivers on the road…to let people know what life on the road is all about."

"Really?" replied the woman with noticeable interest. She asked Sport some questions and then told her to wait and she would find someone.

While she was gone, Sport glanced anxiously around to see if her pursuers might have figured out where she went. She intended to trick them by leaving her car behind and pick it up later.

Soon, Sport was climbing into a truck cab with a young, red-haired man who had the fresh-scrubbed appearance of a college student, although he had to be a few years older. He told her that his name was "G.W." He seemed happy that someone was taking an interest in his life. Sport began with questions about his philosophy of living and his desire to earn big money for a while.

"Life on the road doesn't cost me much more than food, gas and truck maintenance," G.W. explained, "and I am well compensated for my expenses. I don't have rent or mortgage or any other debt. Many nights I can just sleep in my truck and later use shower facilities in the truck stops. I'm trying to build a nest egg for when I'm older and know more about what I want in life and who I want to spend it with."

As they talked, the eighteen wheels whirled and the truck bounced and jolted its riders. Sport glanced several times in the side mirror to see if anyone was following, but the bumps soon took her mind off the dark road behind. The truck wasn't a new version of traveling vehicle.

It had been a long day for Sport, and after about a half hour of conversation, even the unsettling rhythm of truck bounces could not defeat her drowsiness. G.W. suggested that she crawl up in the berth and sleep for a while. For a moment, Sport hesitated, but then she agreed that it would be a welcome rest which she could use. She pulled her one piece of luggage into a corner, put her black coat over her weary body and fell asleep.

But a CB call broke the monotony of the road noise and awakened her partially. She heard the voice ask, "Are you running legal or illegal?"

G.W. didn't answer, and Sport might have dozed for one more round of night driving. Then the CB woke her again when it blared, "I smell skunk!"

Her sleepy mind wondered, *Is this some sort of game?* She thought about the men in the green car earlier, and the subsequent thought was natural: *Are we being followed?*

She called down to G.W., "Where are we now?"

"Don't know exactly," he replied. "I missed my turn."

"Can we stop before long to go to the bathroom?"

"Nope, there is nowhere out here to pull over this rig!"

"Okay, I'll wait a while," Sport answered.

She remembered all the years of having qualms about asking a man to stop on the road so she could go to the bathroom. She certainly could remember the emotional traumas she had suffered and the embarrassment of asking, being refused and its consequences.

*I will have to wait.*

But in a little while the press of urgency made her call out, "How much longer until we can stop?"

"Not for a while!" G.W. answered. He seemed stressed.

Suddenly, creative problem solving had to go into gear. There was no waiting time left. Sport was in a jam. She tossed off the black coat that she had been using as a blanket. She carefully took off her white poplin jacket with the plaid lining. She realized that she was risking the driver raising the flap of the sleeping berth to receive the shock of his life.

*Don't worry about that! I have to do this now!* she urged herself. So, the project began.

*Oh, God! A dam never broke without a lot of pressure, and this one is out of control!* Sport realized. The flood gates were nowhere to be closed; the jacket was not nearly sufficient to contain it; and the mattress received the flow. It seemed like the whole world was in the great flood.

*Even Noah wouldn't have answers for this,* Sport sighed to herself with consternation. She considered whether it would dry before she had to admit the truth to G.W. But the reckoning moment came suddenly when G.W. announced, "I'm going to have to pull off the road and get some sleep. Maybe you can use the bathroom out there."

*God, what awful timing!*

"G.W., I think I better tell you, it's a little wet back here."

"Are you sure?"

Sport sighed. "Positive!"

"Well, I'll turn the mattress over. I have to get some sleep!"

She climbed to the front of the cab. It helped to turn her face away from the situation at hand. She made apologies, but the necessary could not be helped.

But when G.W. was in the berth, he called to her, "How about coming back and getting some sleep? I won't bother you."

She was still trying to find a comfortable curled-up position in the cab with her tall body. But she answered him, "No, I'm fine. That last sleep was a big help!"

"Sure? Maybe you could come back here and let your wildest fantasies take over!"

"No, I'm fine. It's better that you get some sleep anyway," Sport answered.

He was silent for a couple of minutes, and then he said, "You know, I thought you were a real lady when I first saw you. Well, good night!"

Sport felt a smile break out on her face. She had survived the ordeal of the great flood, and she could still talk to the young stranger in the bunk behind her. *We're all human,* she thought, *and strangers can become friends, if even for just a few hours.*

There were lights from a car illuminating the front of the truck. Sport pulled her black coat up over her head and shrunk a little deeper into the seat. She thought in the light that she had momentarily seen a building, but within instants she was asleep.

Finally, it became light, and the long night was over. Sport's clothes had dried. She really needed to wash her face and comb her hair. She reached behind her into the berth and touched G.W. on the

60

arm. He didn't move. She shook his arm again, and he still didn't move. She tried calling his name, repeatedly becoming louder, but he was impervious to her shaking and calling. She had never seen anyone sleep so hard. But with one last violent shaking of his arm, she roused him enough to let him know that she was going into the restaurant that he had parked behind.

She climbed down the six feet or so from the truck cab and proceeded across the parking lot. She hoped that she could make herself look more daytime presentable. She saw that the restaurant was for interstate journeyers. In the traveler's lobby were red curtains everywhere. Sport found it to be a colorful awakening for her own sleepy re-entry into reality. She washed her face and felt a bit more like Thursday morning. Her vacation was turning, spinning and moving faster than she had ever imagined.

Sport didn't like the feel of the dining room, so she returned to the truck and renewed her efforts to bring G.W. to life. It took a lot of prodding, but finally he sat up, looking dazed. His eyes were puffy with a bit of crusted sleep.

"Can we get out of here, please?" Sport asked him. "It's not really nice in there."

G.W. muttered, "Okay, just let me go in and get a Sprite to go." He climbed down from the truck and ambled across the parking lot. As she watched him, Sport realized how thirsty she was and wished that she had asked him for one. But he returned five minutes later, two giant Sprites in hand. Without saying anything, he handed her one and then got behind the wheel.

Despite his courtesy, Sport had a different feeling from G.W. this morning. He seemed almost angry. *Well, maybe he is not so happy about his mattress*, she allowed. As they continued down the road, on a toll road now, G.W. kept silent. Sport decided that she would climb back into the berth for a little more rest, given the mood in the cabin. For some reason, she also didn't want to be seen by the toll collectors when they stopped. So, she got in the berth. She remembered the question from the night before on the CB:

"Are you riding legal or illegal?"

*Could it be that a passenger such as she would make them be riding illegal*, she wondered?

Sport halfway dozed enough to make time pass like sleep, but she was also semi-conscious of sounds in the truck and on the highway. G.W. turned the CB on, and Sport picked up snippets of conversation between spells of dozing:

"Yeah, they said that everything was to be given to a children's foundation."

"It's really something."

"He's getting married today, and he's coming with the rock. A quick service, then they'll be taking off!"

"It's too bad that she'll never get to see her grandson."

She felt a questioning about what was going on, but not strongly enough to pull completely out of sleep. A fantasy came to her that she would be meeting her "St. George" in the town at the end of this run, but she didn't know exactly where they would soon be arriving.

Then the CB said, "Stash the trash and then the name of her school."

That woke her up! She climbed back into the front seat. Outside, it seemed as if the cars and trucks were traveling as if there were no speed laws. G.W. was still silent.

"What has happened?" Sport asked him. "Everyone is driving so fast! And look! There are men working on the highway, really working, and people are hardly slowing."

G.W. acknowledged her statement with a glance out the window, but he still didn't say anything. She thought that perhaps she should write an article about how life on the road affects the mood of a person. She realized that she was affected by strange things seen quickly in the field of view as the truck rushed by. She found herself staring at another example of that: Just ahead on the right, inside a giant rectangle of cinderblocks, "Old Glory" was blowing in the wind. But the flag was tattered and torn, and its spastic movements made it appear as if it were alive and crying for freedom from its imprisonment and neglect. Sport shuddered at that conception, and she put her hands to the "Patriot's Pass" that she was wearing, a movement to comfort herself. But, just over a hill, were three wooden crosses standing starkly in the mid-morning light.

*Easter is just over, but those crosses are there all year*, Sport thought. The three symbols surprisingly made her feel apprehensive. She thought about the little church with the artificial flowers earlier and the emotion seeing that had stirred in her. She realized, suddenly, why she was feeling strange: *Things previously held sacred are no longer valued. The world is changing rapidly, and not for the better.*

Finally, G.W. spoke: "We'll be in my drop-off town shortly. After I unload, I will be going right back. Do you want to return with me, or are you moving on?" Sport thought for a moment and decided that she would return with him, pick up her car, and go home. She would be back in time for school on Monday morning.

It was about 11:30 a.m. when they arrived in the east side of town. He had received directions in the town via the citizens-band radio about where to unload his cargo. Sport observed as they pulled in the parking lot of a terminal that it was overrun with litter and debris. G.W. stopped the truck, got out his ledger book for transacting business and left Sport in the cab. She stared at a family having a picnic in a grassy area to the side. She was incredulous.

*This is the garbage spot of the world! How could they be eating here in such a place?*

She thought that the little girl sitting with a milkshake looked absolutely beautiful. It reminded her that she still had some goodies that the professor had given her, but she didn't want to nibble here! She watched and wondered why the family was there, and what did they normally do?

When G.W. came back to the truck, he seemed agitated. He stared at Sport a few moments through the side window, and then he climbed into the driver's seat and began to do some paperwork. But he apparently became frustrated. He tore off a couple of sheets of yellow paper, wadded them into balls, and threw them towards Sport.

"It's going to get dirty," he told her. To Sport, his actions felt like anger.

*He's treating me like trash*, she thought with an inner shudder.

G.W. began to inch the truck towards the warehouse vehicle entrance. Sport had never been inside such a place, nor had she seen equipment being unloaded, so she sat up fully awake and watched in wonder. G.W. paused at the entrance long enough to hand some papers to a guard, and then he rolled the rig inside. Sport saw neatly stacked container boxes everywhere and massive mashing and packaging equipment. The noise was deafening. She was wondering how the workers could bear hearing that all day, every day, when her eyes caught sight of numerous giant dumpsters with a big number 13 painted on each in yellow. A sense of impending doom suddenly seized her. She felt it in every core of her being, down to the very marrow of her bones. She quickly grabbed her purse, opened the cab of the truck, made a giant jump down and took off running through the warehouse! The sunlight outside greeted her with the monsters of number 13, and she felt that she had escaped just in time.

Sport didn't watch television, so she wasn't sure why the image of G.W. as a bounty hunter popped into her head. Maybe her imagination was in high gear, she thought, but the fear was real.

*If there is any money on my head, they are ready to collect!*

The only thing that mattered to her then was that she felt she needed to get out of there. She ran along a path beside a fence in a hurry to get away from the warehouse. She didn't look back to see if her escape had been noticed. In the distance, she saw small box-like houses.

*If I can just get to the street, I can work my way back to the freeway and get out of East Side.*

Miserably thirsty, she intended first to find someone who could give her a drink of water. Finally, she saw a woman emptying trash.

*How appropriate!* she mused. She hurried before the woman could disappear inside the back of the building. She approached her with a smile.

"Sorry to bother you, but I'm dying of thirst. Would you be able to give me some water?"

The woman answered indifferently, "I don't live here. I just work here. Can't get you a drink of water."

For the first time since Sport's adventure began, she felt like crying, but there wasn't time for the luxury of a breakdown.

*Certainly, in the span of the next few blocks, I'll find a drink of water,* she reassured herself.

But she never saw anyone to ask. She spotted an American flag flying on a small house in the distance. She was certain that good citizens who lived there would give her a drink! Hot now, she made her way there. The house looked boarded. It was up on cinderblocks, but there were no steps to the front door.

*Strange! It's like a mockery...freedom flying and, yet, no entrance!*

Sport remembered having seen a sign for a college on the freeway. She surmised that it was located next to the exit they had taken to come into town. She summoned her physical will and paced her way through some lowland dwelling areas to the freeway. Finally, she heard its traffic. She saw a high embankment that she ascended and got a view of it. But behind her, below, she heard two men calling for her.

"Come on down, and we'll take you to another town," one shouted.

Sport called back, "Pick me up on the freeway!" She wasn't going to trust them, and it would take them some time to arrive at that point on the interstate.

"Come down!" the man called again.

Sport descended the other side of the hill, swung her legs over the interstate rails, observed the traffic a couple of minutes, and then started walking backwards with her thumb extended to the traffic traveling east. But the cars and trucks just kept rolling by her. No one seemed to care that she was out there.

*Geez, what an enlightenment this is!* Sport thought. *Here I am, an educated woman, alone on the side of a freeway. Maybe I'm sleep-deprived, hungry, and thirsty, but, all things considered, I don't look too badly worn. How scary can I be? No one is stopping. No one cares!*

She decided that the best thing to do (even if she had to walk) was to find the college, get something to eat and drink, find a place to stay overnight, and then make her plans to get back to her car.

*At least no one is following me now!*

After a couple miles, Sport realized that on the other side of the interstate was a nearby park. The traffic was heavy and fast, but, trusting her good running shoes, she darted across to the greenery of the other side. There was a wire fence she had to climb. Thankfully, it had no barbed wire on the top. She got her bearings and surmised that she needed to walk at a forty-five-degree angle to the northeast to arrive at the college. It was conjecture, but she trusted her instincts. Getting her feet a little wet in the slushy terrain of grass and mud created by recent rain squalls, Sport headed in that direction. After ten minutes, she began to realize that the college might still be some distance. She remembered that she had a little bit of the muffins left in her purse. She paused to conserve her energy, using the time to moisten her lips and eat a few crumbs.

Starting off again, she crossed some land where dogs tied to ropes attached to trees barked frantically to be set loose to go along with her. Those were her only live welcoming friends so far in the East Side. Eventually, her course towards the college led her into a thicket of thorny forest sub-brush. She wondered how she might get through, but then she saw a stream that offered a path of easier walking. She trudged on.

Suddenly, she heard the noisy approach of dump trucks, although she couldn't see them. Her experiences with people on the East Side not being so friendly thus far, Sport decided that it would be best not to be seen. She abandoned the stream, moved a little way into the scratchy thicket and stretched out on the ground. The sounds came closer and then stopped. She recognized the noise of trash moving up into the truck. Those were sounds that she remembered from back home. She wondered what they were grinding and smashing. She hoped it wasn't her luggage and leather coat that she had left in G.W.'s truck. In the luggage, also, was her most cherished possession: the diplomas. Now these would be gone forever.

She waited for the trucks to move away, and then she heard one very loud buzzer. Sport had heard that sound many times over the years at ball games. Now she knew that she was fairly close to an athletic field. One buzz. To her it meant, "You won!"

She sat up and took off her purple blouse and set it on the ground so that she could lie on it. Now she didn't have any coat or jacket to keep her warm when it became cool. The ground was damp from winter cold, but lying still on the ground, she discovered that the sun was warming her skin. She was at the point of ending her rest time when the trucks returned and the noise began again. She stayed motionless, and when the trucks left again, there was the buzzer once more!

*Round two, I won again!* she thought to herself with a smile.

She checked her watch. A half hour had passed since the first truck visit. She thought that maybe the trucks came at half hour intervals. Relaxing, she nibbled on some of her remaining crumbs and then decided to take a nap. The trucks didn't return. Apparently, all the trash had been ground for the day. Off and on she was half-asleep. Nevertheless, time moved ahead in spurts of unconscious speed, the birds stopped flying and singing, the sky grew very dark, and she dreamed a wonder if the world were about to end.

But…not really! Sport jolted awake. It was still light. The dump trucks had returned! Again, she lie perfectly still, arms crossed over her bra so that no one might see the slightest bit of bright white in the sunlight. The buzzer sounded again, but this time three buzzes. She checked her watch. It was four p.m.

*Get ready, let's go!* Sport thought to herself. The nap and time had emboldened her to take action and leave her tight spot. She needed action now to occupy her mind. It would be getting dark before long.

Sport didn't want the inconvenience of carrying her purse through the thicket, so she thoughtfully chose items she would need the most and put them in her jeans pockets. Even her sunglasses would be a liability in the thicket, so she decided to leave them. Leaning her purse on a little bush, Sport started moving again with the little plastic bag of food in one hand and a walking stick in the other. She wondered if she would ever see the purse again. She cut her path through nasty briers that left some scratches on her skin. Finally, out of the thicket and into a clearing, she climbed an embankment and saw on the other side an old shopping center and parking lot. She walked up to a young man on a motor scooter and asked him directions to the college. She even asked him if he would take her there, but he answered, "Sorry, I'm waiting for my girlfriend to come out of the shop."

The young man's directions would send Sport several blocks to the left and then a left turn on a thoroughfare for additional walking. So, she decided to continue the diagonal trek to cut some distance and time. She didn't want to admit to herself that her journey to the college had become a marathon of hiking endurance.

It became obvious to her that she was still in East Side when she came to the biggest parking lot for trash trucks that she had ever seen. She skirted it and went to the street. In the distance, she saw a big building that looked like it might belong on the college campus, so she headed in that direction. It turned out to be a private school where the children were enjoying a soccer tournament.

*At least there's life and children in this town as it nears six o'clock!* she told herself.

At last she found the campus! She walked over a hill and sat on the ground under a tree to rest a few minutes. She asked a young man where the girls' residence hall was. She followed his directions to the front door of the building and knocked. When no one answered, she opened the door and went into a large entry room. Several young women were gathered around a piano where one was playing. She asked them if the house mother was in.

"She's out to dinner. It could be a while before she gets back," one answered.

Sport looked at her reflection in a glass that protected a wall painting. *I really need to shower and make myself presentable before I meet the house mother to ask if I can spend the night,* she decided.

She addressed the girls again. "Could you tell me if anyone has an extra towel and washcloth that I might wash up with in a shower? I have been hiking over Easter vacation. I'm a mess. I really can't meet your housemother looking like this!"

One of the young ladies looked at Sport with eyes that fathomed her need. She told Sport to follow her.

Sport soon found herself in a shower. *Oh, the pleasure of a clean washcloth, soap and towel!* The water felt completely wonderful, even if it was only lukewarm and light in water pressure on her aching muscles. It was sheer pleasure!

After giving her jeans a smudge-rub job to remove the mud, Sport got back into her clothes. She told the young college co-ed that she had on her first pair of jeans and that she usually wore suits to school when she taught. The woman smiled and handed Sport some face and hand cream.

*What a joy to find this young good Samaritan in East Side,* she thought happily. She felt renewed. An impulse stirred in her.

Sport went downstairs and found phone booths. She called her precious Saint George.

He said, "I've been trying to reach you!"

"I'm sorry, I'm so very sorry," Sport answered. She asked him if he still loved her.

There was a pause, and he said, "I can't hurt others. I have to be where I am."

And, for all their eight years of dreams, that was the reply. She slowly replaced the receiver as his only advice hung in her ear: "Regroup!"

She leaned against the wall.

*Well, I have certainly been doing that all day! How did he know?*

She made one other call which went to an answering machine. She left a simple message: "I'm okay."

She still had her credit card, so she should be able to get out of the town and return home. Back in a lounge near the house-mother's room, Sport spotted a blanket folded on the back of a sofa. She took it and curled up under it on the sofa and fell asleep.

There was a skip of time, and then suddenly someone pulled the blanket from her.

"Are you alright?" In Sport's awakening brain, the voice was soft at first, but it quickly became urgent and demanding. "You can't be sleeping here! Who are you? Why are you here? How did you get here? You can't stay here!"

Sport sat up and suddenly felt ill. She knew why. She interrupted the woman's high intensity demands and told her, "Hold up! I've got high blood pressure and need my medication."

"But what are you doing here?"

"Please, quit shouting. Just call a rescue squad for me. I need to get to a hospital. I feel that my blood pressure is very high," Sport pleaded.

Time seemed to pass quickly in Sport's feeling of disorientation. The next thing that she knew, a man from administration and a campus security policeman were examining her driver's license. They told her that the ambulance was on the way. The visit to the college was not going as Sport had envisioned it at all. She had wanted to come to find a quiet night's sleep, but everything had become pandemonium.

Then, suddenly, there was a change of attitude. The house mother and the man from administration had disappeared a few minutes, but when they returned, the house mother had for Sport a bowl of watermelon and cantaloupe. The man handed her an orange juice.

Incredulously, the woman said, "If we had known you were coming, we would have set a place for you."

The security guard smiled, and he asked her, "Were you in Irvine, California in 1967?"

The question was very strange, and it shocked Sport into a memory. She remembered standing before a customs man in his smart white uniform. She had returned from a stay in Hong Kong with her husband. On the way over, she had been taken on a polar

69

route, but the return included a stop in the Hawaiian Islands. The customs man had said to her, "Good morning, Sport, did you and your husband have a nice stay in Hong Kong, and did he get off the ship alright?"

And now this security man was asking her if she had been in Irvine in 1967!

"Why, yes!" Sport answered him.

It was a year that she would always remember. She had left California to be in Hong Kong with her husband when he received his military orders to be stationed there.

*How do they know here in East Side where I had been in 1967? Who is keeping track of me? What data base am I in?*

She turned to the man in administration who seemed to be in charge of things. "You probably have a better resume of me than I have!"

He smiled faintly.

She told him, "Well, then I challenge you to put me in a college network system that will allow me to travel all over the United States to visit college campuses! I would like to observe what is going on in education."

The man didn't seem surprised by Sport's reaction. He said, "Well, what direction do you want to go?"

Sport felt both playful and angry. Her head still was woozy. She told him, "Oh, I would zig-zag all over the country: north, south, east, west…"

But the conversation continued as if it were plausible for the man to grant Sport access to colleges nationwide by putting her credentials in a computer system. She apparently was already in some system.

*I am sure that these people found out something about me that changed their attitude toward me,* she thought. *Will I find out what?*

She asked for the man's card. She would remember him. She wanted to ask him more.

But the paramedics arrived.

# Chapter 7: The Naked Edges

The paramedics arrived at the college and began questioning Sport like a college professor's final examination. Answer a., b., c., d., all of the above. She told them, "Please just take my blood pressure first! It feels so high!" They put the cuff on her arm and watched the needle move with starts and stops. She asked them what the reading was, and when they told her, she said, "That's too high for me! I need my blood pressure medicine. I lost the medication I had with me for the trip. I am supposed to take it three times a day; otherwise, the doctor said I could have a heart attack! The dosage has been reduced recently. I had to stop taking a new kind of medicine, because it was making me dizzy."

The paramedics bundled her onto a stretcher and took her out of the residence hall. The lights inside the rescue vehicle were as bright as those in an operating room. Someone asked her hospital of preference. Sport had heard someone say that a small hospital nearby had a Doctor of Osteopathy. Therefore, she requested that particular hospital. She had had a back injury that bothered her somewhat, so she thought that doctor and hospital would be good choices for her.

But when they arrived at the hospital and opened the rear doors of the vehicle, which let in the fresh air, Sport saw the sign with the hospital's name and realized that she had been brought to the wrong one. She asked why they had gone there. The driver replied, "We just assumed…"

"No," Sport interrupted, "I want to go to the one where the Osteopath has privileges."

There was no disagreement, so they all returned to their places inside the ambulance and headed to the other hospital. By this time, Sport's blood pressure had dropped to what was a high normal for her. She remembered her family doctor telling her, "You are one of the few people I know who can sit quietly for a few minutes and your blood pressure drops significantly."

She had thought at the time, *I think my meditations are the secret for blood pressure control.* She sighed. *I just want to be seen, get my medications, and get out of here.*

In the hospital, Sport was rushed into a white gown which was short and button-less. She felt very much on view. The gown reduced her shape, she felt, to a zero on a scale of zero to ten.

*Well, I've never been a ten in anyone's book, so it doesn't really matter,* she told herself.

A nurse with a kind voice took her temperature and other vital signs. After a while the doctor arrived. After a few questions, he escorted Sport to the elevator. A loud-mouthed, talkative patient waited in the hall with them. He filled the air with all kinds of floating information, like the fact that he was a taxi driver and that his company accepted credit cards. At that moment, however, Sport didn't want to hear his voice. She just wanted her medication so she could feel better. She was not particularly polite to the man. When the elevator arrived, she and the doctor got on and rode to the third floor, where the doctor had his treatment room. In it was a table for manipulations.

"Your table doesn't have a split where your face is supposed to fit," she pointed out to Dr. Warm. It's not like the table that my doctor back home has. Where did you take your training?"

He responded, and Sport said, "Oh, that's a good school."

Carefully, the doctor worked on her back. He told Sport that he did not do shoulder or neck manipulations. She recalled a long time previously in Los Angeles when she had allowed a doctor who was not an osteopath to work on her neck. It had been a doctor whom she did not know. He had given her more than enough treatment that day. She had begun to see psychedelic, colored lights. That had been a frightening experience, and she didn't need anything like that now. So, she thanked Dr. Warm for his services when he was done. They went back down to the first-floor emergency room. He gave her a three-day supply of medicine and a prescription. When she was dismissed, she asked, "How can I get to a nice motel here in East Side?"

"You can call a cab," suggested the woman at the desk.

*But I don't have any cash nor checks to write for cab fare*, Sport thought. She thought about the loud-mouthed taxi driver and wished that she had paid more attention to his ramblings. She would have to think of something else to work out.

Sport went to the nurse's station to ask if any of them might be going back into town.

"Sorry," the nurse explained. "The other shift just left. Everyone has gone home. We are just starting our shift. I am afraid that you can't stay here."

She left the hospital. The night air was chilled by the sprinkling of a cold rain. She longed for her white jacket even if it was filthy. Anything would add a touch of welcome warmth. She didn't even want to remember her black leather Avanti coat. That had long been lost in the world of the unknown.

A black New Yorker with plush red velvet interior drove up. Sport hailed it, and the woman passenger rolled down her window. The man stared straight ahead. The woman answered Sport with directions to a motel on Water Street. While she was talking, Sport imagined herself being chauffeured in a car like that. She might be dressed elegantly instead of the way she was now. What a contrast! She had a remorseful feeling about a time that she had eluded money that she should have accepted. Even though once she had known good times, she had never known a car like this. But she saw a couple blocks away the corner of Water Street, where the motel was lit. She thanked the woman for her kindness.

In the motel office, the registration clerk was a tall young man with a speech impediment and, perhaps, a disconnection of brain synapses. Somehow, they managed the registration.

"Do you have a room where the windows will open?"

"Yes," he answered and handed her the key to room 104. He then disappeared into a back office.

She went to the room, unlocked the door, flipped the light switch on and leaned for a few moments against the doorframe. She was exhausted. She could not even calculate how long it had been since she had slept well in a real bed. After a fast shower, she opened the window in the room, decided to leave the bathroom light on, and then she crashed into bed. She would solve the problems of getting clean clothes and getting home in the morning. She collapsed into a sleep.

But it was still dark when Sport awoke with a start! She felt suffocating and lethargic.

*There's not enough oxygen in this room!*

When she sat up, her head spun with dizziness. She waited to become steadier, then she went to the window that she had opened and parted the drapes. She discovered to her horror a wall outside the window within two feet of her. The muggy air was stifling; the wall blocked fresh air currents. Looking upward where heaven was supposed to be, she saw in the narrow view of the sky a few stars informing that the night was clear. Her room was actually below street level.

*What lies beyond the wall? The river?*

She went to the phone and called St. George.

"I'm ready to negotiate," she said. "I need a traveling companion. I'm on the right, and you're on the left. I'll bend a little to the middle, and you can bend, and then we will command the whole road."

He laughed and said, "I can't bend!"

*Yes,* she thought, *we are a pair who can play mind games and boggle even the best.*

Despite her predicament, Sport laughed and answered, "Well, when you decide to change your mind, just let me know. I'm fast. I travel light and come out quick!"

He also laughed. Somehow, even though her earlier conversation with him in the evening had made her sad, his laughter then made everything better.

Except for the feeling of suffocation that re-asserted itself.

She went to the lobby desk and rang the desk bell several times until the young man emerged sleepily from the back room. He wasn't in a good mood, and he couldn't find her another room that would have fresh air.

"I'll sit here until morning!" Sport told him. She saw a small refrigerator in the area where continental breakfast would be served later. She felt the young man staring at her back as she retrieved a small carton of orange juice from it. She was feeling dizzy, so she plopped in a chair and gulped the juice as quickly as she could.

From the desk, the young man told her, "You can't stay in the lobby!"

But Sport felt flushed. "Call an ambulance, police, fire department…any of them! I feel really sick and need some care."

The police arrived and took her back to the same hospital that she had left earlier. The questions came in droves: "Are you here alone? Do you have family nearby? What are you doing here? Where have you been staying?"

She tried to fill them in that she was traveling on Easter vacation, that she originally had intended to be writing a book on her trip but that she had run into some problems, and now she needed to feel better and return home.

This was a different group of nurses. They attached her to a constantly monitoring blood pressure machine and then left, busy with patients. But the cuff kept strengthening its grip on her arm. It quickly started to hurt. She called to the nurse please to come and release the cuff.

From the door, the nurse looked and said, impatiently, "I can see it. There's nothing wrong with it. It's alright."

She started to walk away, but Sport insisted, "No! Please, come take it off. It's too tight. It has been on too long, and I can't stand it!"

The nurse snarled as she came back in the room. "It's a machine. It's working fine. There's nothing wrong with it."

She was almost in tears as she realized: *This machine is a robot, but so is this nurse!* Continuing to insist, Sport finally succeeded in getting the nurse to remove the cuff.

The doctor at last appeared, and it was Dr. Warm again. He checked vital signs and examined her and admitted that he did not know what was wrong with her yet.

"I must always have fresh air," she explained. "The motel room didn't have fresh air." She saw that the doctor's expression was skeptical. "I have had this problem for years. I get weak and dizzy when there is recycled air in buildings. If it's bad, I can faint! And I can tell that even in this hospital, there is recycled air."

The doctor looked as if he were taking Sport's comment personally. "There isn't anything wrong with the hospital air!" He made a note in her chart. It seemed that he had turned into Dr. Cold. He tried to mask impatience as he glanced at his watch. It was four a.m.

"We'll find a place for you to get some rest," he told her. He was trying to sound concerned for her.

Sport acted like she believed his interest in her well-being. "Thank you!" she said.

"In the next town, Sinbad, there is a hospital that you may find more suitable. We are small here. I will arrange for an ambulance to transfer you."

But while they awaited the transport, the doctor did a few more things. He checked her reflexes, and then he shone a light into her eyes. Sport knew that her vision was twenty-twenty, but the doctor was temporarily blinding her with the light. In the background the nurses continued working somewhere. To Sport, the blinding by the doctor seemed symbolic, as if he didn't want her to see the truth.

When the paramedics arrived with a stretcher for her, Sport asked if she could walk out to the vehicle. She didn't wait for their answer, certain to be negative, and she went out into the early-morning-fresh air. It felt like freedom and relief. At the door to the ambulance, she allowed the stretcher that she would use for the ride. Lying down, she felt the nurturing of the clean sheets, and she asked for the additional comfort of a blanket, which a paramedic got for her. As they started the trip, they inserted tubing into her nostrils to connect her to an oxygen tank. In no time, she realized that she was only receiving residues of gas.

"Your oxygen tank is empty!" Sport told them.

Examining it, a paramedic looked sheepish and admitted that it was.

"It's okay," Sport told him. "I'm grateful for the blanket."

They got on the interstate. She felt and heard the wheels rolling hard. She remembered G. W. and his green and white truck that had taken her to such drastic places. Then a recognizable odor came to her nose, which had been freed from the tubing.

"I smell burning rubber. You better check your tires!" she shouted to the men in the front.

A young man named Bud took a seat beside her. "Yeah, you could be right. I told them earlier that they had overinflated the tires when they put air in. I guess they are running hot."

Sport asked if the air-conditioning could be turned up in the back with outside air coming in. She became a little more relaxed as Bud seemed talkative and told her something of his life. He was in serious financial trouble. His wife didn't work, and, worse, she wanted to divorce him and get the house and most of his salary. He worked his job at least eighty hours per week. He went on and on with his problems. As he talked, Sport observed his bloodshot eyes and fatigued shoulders. She felt sorry for him. He could not have been more than twenty-five years old and so heavily burdened. In the time of the journey, Sport and the young man bonded. She felt like

76

she had met a son. He held her hand and promised not to leave her at the next hospital unless she were satisfied with the situation.

They rolled in at the first stretches of dawn arising and fog wrapping the fountain in front of the big colonial building. It looked welcoming. Sport was surprised that they were to enter the front of it. She felt that she could walk, and they ascended the steps to the large front doors and went in a mildew-ridden building of ancient means. A nurse met them at the door to a vestibule. She said that she would take Sport to get a drink that she had requested. She opened one of two large double doors, and they all walked into a lobby with ceilings that exceeded fifteen feet. Her drink was at a water fountain. Sport gulped a full minute, and all the while she could not shake misgivings that had come suddenly upon her.

*I don't find any peace in this place!* she thought to herself.

The nurse escorted them to a back office down the hall.

"Dr. Blue will see you in a few minutes for admittance," she told Sport. She asked for her insurance card for payment purposes.

Sport turned to Bud and asked him to please stay.

Dr. Blue arrived about thirty minutes later. He was a dark-haired man with a thick black moustache and penetrating, deep-brown eyes. Those eyes clearly broadcast displeasure that he had been called out of bed during the early-morning hour. He began pummeling Sport with questions, and he wanted her to sign admission papers in front of him immediately.

She felt her uneasiness growing. Looking around the office, she saw that everything was very makeshift. On the wall were a few notices that hung by scotch tape as if those had not been hanging there for long. She knew how poorly scotch tape adhered to the wall when there were temperature changes. She didn't see holders on the desk containing pens or pencils or paper clips, and no computer terminal. When Dr. Blue opened the desk drawer in front of him, she saw that it was mainly empty. She then fully questioned the whole situation in her mind.

"Just what kind of admittance is this?

The doctor was ruffled by her question.

"It's for evaluations for your well-being."

"And how long would I stay? Who decides this?

"I decide when to recommend your discharge," the doctor answered. "Your case is presented to a judge, who decides in court if you are able to leave."

Sport was appalled. "In other words, one person…you…decides my life, as to whether or not I am ready to be screened by the court?"

The nurse handed her a small glass of apple juice as Dr. Blue answered, "That's right." Sport carefully took a sip and set the glass down.

*Just as I expected: a bitter taste. This has a sedative in it.*

She rose, and turned to Bud. "Take me back to East Side. I'm not staying here. This isn't the kind of rest I need, and no one decides my future for me."

She hadn't eaten much nor had had sufficient sleep, but Sport had mustered all her inner strength to be assertive. Dr. Blue and the nurse looked a bit shocked at the clarity of thought behind Sport's action. As she and Bud left, her thought was, *Geez, they were trying to admit me into a state mental institution! This is one more stigma I have to put behind me.*

Back in the ambulance, Sport sat and talked in confidence with Bud. He told her, "I'll try to help you find a place to stay today. My pastor might help you find a place with food and rest for a day or two. We have to take you back to East Side Hospital. When we get there, I will get his address and phone number for you."

"Can't you just let me off at a motel along the way?" Sport asked him.

Bud laughed. "No, we're liable. We have to transport you to hospitals. It's the law. But, don't worry. We'll figure something out when we get back."

Sport thought about hospitals and realized that one couldn't enter or exit them without proper procedures and signature forms. They arrived back at East Side Hospital, and Sport found her freedom in an odd way:

She asked directions to a restroom while the ambulance crew went to a hospitality area for snacks and while Bud went off in search for a phone book that might have the number and address of his pastor. She came out and sat in a waiting room and watched a change in nursing shifts. Some of the nurses were dressed in light colored jeans instead of the formal white uniforms. They looked much more comfortable than the nurses in white. She was waiting for Bud to return when a woman came out from the triage area and told Sport that there was no necessity for her being there.

"You have to leave," she told Sport. "We can't house the homeless in our waiting rooms."

Sport was surprised and instantly arose to exit. Apparently, she headed toward the wrong door.

"Not that one!" said the nurse, who was still watching her. "The door over there."

And that was how Sport found the electric doors that opened to her Friday morning freedom! It was a different entrance from the one she had entered, so there was no ambulance and crew waiting for her. Sport made her way to the end of the driveway and came to a main road that had some traffic.

*What direction might downtown be?* she wondered. *I need to find a store like Penny's and get some fresh clothes, but right now the main thing is I need some breakfast!*

She thought about sweet Bud and wished that she could say goodbye. She decided that she would call the ambulance service later and let him know how grateful she was for his help. She wanted to keep connected with the one person on her journey who seemed to care what happened to her.

Sport noted her low energy level. *For now, until I eat, I should conserve my energy*, she said to herself.

She walked slowly. Within a few blocks, she saw a lovely church and wondered if it would be open early on a Friday morning. She walked up to the front doors, which were, of course, locked, but the green welcome mat left her with a good feeling. She strolled around the side of the church to the back and came upon trash cans. Remembering the yellow dumpsters at the warehouse, Sport shuddered. A crop of pine trees in the rear of the property offered shelter from the gentle rain that had started falling. She huddled underneath their protective branches on the ground. Her purple blouse was now wet and cold.

*These trees are the only protection I have felt recently,* Sport thought sadly. *I definitely am outside all normal systems these past few days. A true outsider.* She shuddered again, this time from the damp cold. *I set out on my vacation to find out the condition of the world in which I live. I left the inclusiveness of my lovely classroom, my job, my friends, my family. And, suddenly, I'm a nobody in a strange town where no one cares about me. The consistent feelings I receive are that I don't belong, I can't stay, and I must leave.* She sighed. *At least I can comb my hair, wash my face and hold onto my credit card.*

It was the mid-nineteen eighties. She had recently read a clipping in a small college newspaper that people were attempting to travel only on plastic money clear across the country. She was pretty much doing the same thing now!

*It's definitely possible, but better to have a little cash for taxis and tidbit needs.*

The rain slackened. Much of the traffic seemed to be moving in the direction towards town, so she decided to walk to town also. It surprised her sometimes, the things that she noticed. She felt observant, and that was an advantage when she played "Mastermind." As she walked, she thought to herself: *The people who live in these houses must either sleep or watch television all the time. I never see anyone come out, not even to get the morning paper. What is happening in the world? Have all the unhappiness and meanness been occurring for some time and I never noticed until this trip? Why are people so closed up?*

A bit down the road, Sport found a gasoline service center that sold convenience items, including coffee and snacks. She asked the Asian man if the store accepted credit cards. He nodded, "Yes." She went first to the restroom, where she washed her face, combed her hair, and applied some makeup. She checked herself in the mirror.

*Not too bad considering the type of living I've been doing lately,* she laughed to herself.

She purchased a honey bun, crackers, coffee and a mug for carrying water. She washed the mug and filled it from the bathroom spigot. Certainly, this mug might become her closest ally as the day wore on. Fortified with these supplies, Sport continued down the street until she spotted a nursery with lovely plants and hanging baskets. She wanted to sit on the doorstep of the nursery sales building until it opened, but she worried that might be considered loitering, so she walked to the side where a picnic table was for sale in a spot out of view of the road. She sat and pinched off pieces of the bun and took out a few crackers.

*My little crumbs,* she thought to herself. *Maybe eating like a bird will save my life. What a situation I have been in!*

Afterwards, she began hiking again. She pondered her life. She had always been clever, had always used her brain, had always had to figure out how to act in situations that were alien to her. So much had been! But a lifetime of synthesizing foreign information and putting this together with intuitive knowledge had helped her build an ever-developing reserve of self-reliance. Therefore, when Sport came now to a fork in the road, she looked at it both symbolically and practically. She had to choose going either to the left or the right. She wanted to get to the town to buy some clean clothes. Shutting her eyes, she envisioned the river bank to the right and the freeway to the left.

At that moment, a large German Shepherd nosed her leg, and when Sport opened her eyes in a start, the dog jumped back skittishly and stared. Not certain about his degree of friendliness, Sport offered her closed fist for the dog to smell. He came back cautiously and ignored her hand; instead, he sniffed her jeans.

*Ha! Well, the shit on these jeans is probably giving me lots of protection if this pooch is a bit on the anti-social side,* she thought with a half-smile. After a minute of intense interest, the dog suddenly abandoned her and jogged a short distance away. Then he turned and looked at her as if to say, "Follow me, don't just stand there!"

*Ha! The dog knows a route, neither right nor left, which I don't know,* Sport surmised. Intuition told her to follow the dog. She had to hustle a bit. As it turned out, the dog led her to a place where the river and the freeway intersected. She followed it along the river bank, passing under the overpass of the freeway, until it came to an open field of grass. Then, as if feeling a tsunami of joy, the dog went running across the field.

Sport thought for a moment. The dog was leaving her behind now. It was as if he had wanted to show her this place. She saw that the grass was still early-morning wet.

*That wet clover is going to feel wonderful on my aching feet!*

She took off her shoes and started across. Catching some of the dog's "alegria," Sport started to sing old familiar camp songs that she knew as a child and young teen. The sun had traveled in a clear sky above the distant tree line. Sport heard the dog barking from a distant farmhouse that was partially hidden from her view by a rise of land.

*A bark of invitation! Probably your house, fella, but I have things to do! Thanks for helping me out!*

She came to the school buildings of a bible college. This encouraged her, because she thought that she could find a phone in one of them and get some help on arrangements to return home. It was eight a.m., and, of course, the buildings and dorms were locked. If anyone was in any of them, they must be sleeping. She sat in front of one of the buildings and nibbled a few more crumbs of breakfast. Stretching out her legs in the sun, Sport allowed her feet to dry before putting her shoes on again. She smiled to herself ironically.

*This is really turning out to be a traveling vacation! Well, vacation is not quite adequate to describe this exercise of physical and mental gymnastics!*

Sport remembered seeing a concrete picnic table by the river nearby in a small park that had a map posted in a framed outdoor billboard to show location and hiking trails. She could go there to look at it to get her bearings on her exact location and figure out where to go from there. She strolled to the park and took a seat at the table. The river looked quiet and peaceful, and traffic on the freeway close to it was light this early in the morning. It seemed a good time to rest a while and enjoy the sounds of the birds singing.

But she did not have long before the approaching sound of a car bumping along on the little park dirt road startled her. She saw a lone man driving it. She got up to leave because she didn't feel up to conversation with anyone at that particular moment. Considering some of her hair-raising experiences, being cautious seemed to be the prudent action for her. So, before the man could stop the engine and get out, Sport advanced toward the freeway that was to her left. She didn't have time to look at the map. Climbing a dark brown wooden park fence, she descended a small embankment and made an easy crossing to the other side of the freeway.

*If that guy wanted to follow me in his car, it would take him a while to arrive here,* she thought, satisfied with her evasive action. She didn't want to over-react to things, but she thought it good to be wary in this city called East Side.

An exit road was just a short walk along the highway, and at the end of it was a service station. It was open! Sport decided to go there to use the phone to arrange for a rental car. As she approached, she saw a sign that read, "Manager on Duty."

*Well, I have two quarters remaining. Two phone calls. This could be my last great idea.*

She saw the manager inside and walked up to ask if there was a payphone or if she could use his phone.

*Down to two quarters. Choices! That should be the name of the day.*

She was the one in charge of herself, and the choices were hers to make.

# Chapter 8: Choices

*Making choices means that you have considered all the alternatives and have made a specific decision,* Sport thought to herself. She took the phone book in hand and found a budget car rental and dialed the number carefully. She had been able to save a quarter by explaining her plight to the service station manager. He let her use his phone. *And that is a graciousness that I have rarely encountered on this trip,* Sport observed. It was nice to have positive thoughts again.

The manager at the budget car rental said that someone would come shortly to pick her up and bring her to town to sign the documents for renting the car.

*Yes! I will be closer to the center of town and can finally shop for clean clothes!*

The manager himself was the one who arrived for Sport. He drove quite a distance to the center of East Side and stopped at a car dealership. She commented that she wished she had her own leased car right now so that she wouldn't need to worry the manager about renting the car. Nevertheless, the paperwork began, and suddenly she was told that she would need to decide where she would be driving the car. She would only be allowed to drive within a 200-mile radius of East Side.

*That's strange,* she thought. *I always figured that rental cars could be driven from coast to coast, if need be, and then dropped off.*

The manager began totaling the charges, and, suddenly, these were close to $150 without the car even being driven off the lot. Then, when he phoned in her credit card for approval to cover the charges, Sport's new Waterloo occurred: She had hit her credit limit, and her car rental could not be approved.

*Yikes!* Smiling, she said, "Let me go and do some shopping on the credit limit I have left. I'll make a phone call and get this straight with you later today." But she realized that car rental would be out of her financial thinking.

Stepping out of the small office building, she saw that she was close to the downtown area, and she started walking towards the Penney's store. It was not yet ten a.m., so the downtown was still deserted. There was nowhere to shop or eat, and she couldn't find a working phone booth. She had tried that at the last street corner.

Now Sport had a worry return to her that made her pause: *Am I becoming a street person?* She had read of bag people, street people and run-aways. *Here I am, a respectable teacher on vacation, and I am caught in this crazy drama that feels full of dynamite!*

She caught sight of a couple of elderly ladies who seemed to be enjoying a Friday morning stroll. Liking to talk to people, Sport caught up with them where the road was about to go over a long bridge. She asked them where the road over the bridge led.

"To the next state!" they chimed.

Sport saw the route signs mounted at the start of the bridge and observed that the road was heading south. She really needed to hitch-hike if she were going to make it home in time for Monday classes. Now getting home by then would appear to require some good luck, a short commodity for her lately.

*Time is getting away fast*, she realized. *I really can't wait for Penny's to open at ten a.m.* She had never walked over a big river before on a medium-sized bridge. The idea excited her. She remembered recently telling someone about a dream in which she had fallen from a bridge into peace. She laughed at the memory, because Sport was afraid of both heights and water, but the poetic recalling fit her feelings now.

Saying goodbye to the ladies, Sport prepared to walk the bridge. She checked herself in the now warm, shining sun. Despite rain earlier in the morning, her purple blouse didn't look too wrinkled. She proceeded to the bridge, where she saw strange, block-shaped security signs. Vandals had added cut-out faces to them. One of them had a red eye which peered out into the world, while a face behind it was silent.

*Okay, here we go!* Sport told herself as she started ahead. Along the river on the southern side, the trees were tall. She could hear mechanical equipment working in warehouses in the distance. Otherwise, things were very quiet. People didn't seem to be working anywhere. Another dump-truck passed.

*Geez, this town really has its share of those!* Sport observed.

The road began to wind around a small orchard with apple trees in blossom. This was the first beautiful sight that she had seen in a while, and, suddenly, her day felt orderly and restorative.

The cars whistled by. Trucks honked for her to get out of the way as she started to ascend the busy highway up a miniature mountain. She thought of the "Sound of Music" and the song, "Climb Every Mountain," which seemed to have become a reality for her. At places the highway had a sidewalk which she happily took. The road sign said that she was following Route 7, and that reminded her of the Friendship 7 spacecraft and her recent trip with Christa.

She passed the blossoming apple trees and some straggling daffodils that looked lost in the grass. The sidewalk held its share of glass shards, nails and remnants of moments of previous travelers. The sun was getting very warm. Her little bottle of water taken sip by sip was dwindling. The next order of business became to refill the bottle and then find a payphone to call a friend back home who would help her by moving some finances into her credit card account. She needed clothes!

She spied a store called "Ridges." Inside, Sport found a water fountain. Its cold water was marvelous to her noon-day thirst. She saw a sign that her type of credit card was accepted, so she proceeded to hunt for jeans and a matching jacket. She had had enough of spring travel in these mountains without a jacket or coat. Today still held no promises as to where she might be staying, so she wanted to be prepared for a chilly evening. She was in luck! She found a pair of jeans the right size and a jacket to match, and both were on sale. She decided that her purple blouse could bear up under another day or two of wear. She purchased the items, but when she went back into the dressing room to change into her new clothes, she found that the jeans did not fit her after all. She took them off, put her old ones back on, and refilled her pockets. *What a bother, geez,* she thought with annoyance.

Finding the next larger size, Sport took the jeans to the cashier and asked the girl if she could exchange the smaller pair for the larger. The girl was slow to answer, and a young man working nearby said, "Yeah, it's a good idea to get her approval, because in this town they will have you before a judge in a hurry!" Sport looked at him, thinking that he might be joking, but saw that he was serious. Then he added, strangely, "There's going to be big trouble this afternoon down at the treatment plant." He didn't look at her; he just kept working with his white paint and rollers in the pan.

Sport replied, "Looks like you will be busy here painting!"

"Nope, not me," he answered. "I'm going to be in my big, air-conditioned van, and you might want to be away from here."

"Um…okay, thanks for the advice," Sport replied. She hurried back into the dressing room and changed into her new jean outfit. She threw her old pair into a waste basket.

"Shit!" she said, under her breath. It was a word that she had never brought herself to say until this trip. "I feel like I'm in the Twilight Zone or on some alien planet."

Seeing a phone booth, she called her friend back home, collect. She asked him if he would be able to loan her some money and put it on her credit card. He would need to talk to them and get their agreement that she could use her account. He was doubtful of that possibility.

"It would take time for funds to transfer," he explained. He added, "If I could, I would give you my credit to use, but I don't know if anyone would accept that without plastic or my identification. Besides, I'm pretty much maxed out myself. But I will see what I can do."

So, her hope of a funds transfer diminished, and she only had a small amount of credit remaining. That, and a few crackers in her jeans pocket. Her remaining choice was to start walking Route 7 again and hope for a good ride to come along.

She started out, remembering the young man's warning. She wanted to be far enough away from the treatment plant. *Maybe he will come along in that big air-conditioned van*, she thought, somewhat humorously, but that didn't happen.

As she distanced herself from Ridges, the two-lane highway became a four-lane freeway, and the sidewalk disappeared. Soon she found herself on another bridge high above the river. The odor of chemicals danced around in the shifts of the wind. She had found uneasiness on her adventure and a little bit of fear, but being afraid was never anything that stood in Sport's way of moving on. She felt that she was a free person and that, somehow, she would get home. Just how remained for her to discover.

She stopped and sat on a ledge above the river to rest for a bit and to take a few sips of water. She liked her cup that said, "Super America," and she found comfort in wearing her Patriot's Pass. She thought that it gave her a core of strength that her forefathers had relied upon. *Small things, but they give me confidence,* she thought, *and God knows, on this trip I need that!*

The afternoon became much warmer, so she removed her jacket and carried it. She saw a man hiking on the other side of the road and hoped to get his attention, but he never smiled or waved. She wondered why he was hiking. By this time, Sport had decided that she was hiking for freedom and education.

*Maybe, when this is all over, I can say exactly which choices I made were mistakes,* she told herself then. *I certainly cannot afford to make any more mistakes from this point on. They nearly cost me my freedom in the early hours today and my life yesterday. What a mess! Well, no time to think about that now.*

She needed to get her prescription filled for her medication before she walked out of this state, whichever one it was. She passed several businesses. Everything seemed stone silent except for some trucks idling, but their drivers were nowhere to be seen. She felt as though there were people inside the businesses watching her. She was not sure. It was just her feeling. She hoped to see a truck driver whom she could ask for a ride. She eyed the gravel lot on the right side of a warehouse where trucks would need to exit, but the drivers of two trucks there were not in the vehicles. There was nothing in this place that she could rely upon to help her. She would have to move on.

The left side of the road was more shaded, so Sport thought that would be a better side to walk. Besides, a sign near her said, "Falling Rocks," and the cliff ahead on the right looked shaky. Obviously, prior avalanches had taken their tolls. She imagined earlier centuries when a lone Indian might have stood atop the cliff to decide the best path for him to take. But as she progressed along the road, it became a game to her to walk one side and then the other. She remembered a phone call to a faraway friend who had said to take the whole road in business. So, she did. Anyone watching her might have wondered why she crossed over from time to time. As she walked, Sport did remember the message about the treatment plant, and she wondered what it had to do with her.

In a while, she spotted a highway roadside restaurant ahead on the left side. She was relieved. She wanted to get some ice water, have a late lunch and rest a little. When she walked in, a friendly looking waitress said to her, "I think you'll enjoy sitting here close to the door. If there are any problems, you can get out quick!"

That sounded strange to Sport. *I seem to be in the middle of some local problems of which I don't have a clue what they concern,* she thought. She hurriedly ordered some light food, gave the waitress her card and was out and on her way in less than ten minutes. Her apprehension was becoming as strong as her curiosity about what might be taking place in the area.

Her hike up the road now took her uphill, and at the brow of the next mountain, Sport had a view of the valley in which she could see a few factories. The valley was silent and everything looked immobile.

*This is Friday, right? Why wouldn't the factories be operating today?*

But then she heard a whistle that jolted her into a feeling that she should keep moving. She wondered how far she could go if she walked faster. The highway at this point kept the valley in view. As a mental game, she picked out buildings, intersections and terrain changes as markers for her to switch from one side of the road to the other. She heard more factory whistles, and these started to become a code for her to work in her head, an activity that dispelled any boredom that might fall upon her.

She rested after a while on the step beside a maintenance box on the side of the road where she had a nice view of the valley. There was a factory on top of a hill below. She watched a truck leave it and start down the hill. But the truck made brief stops on one side of the road and then the other, as if offering something to unseen takers standing there. She had an odd thought: What if the truck was delivering money? She could certainly use that!

She got on the move again, and after a while she noticed that a man ahead on a tractor was spraying a hillside lawn with a white chemical. Sport quickly caught the first whiffs of its odor. She drew herself up. She realized that she must not panic. Given her breathing problems, Sport had to keep calm, because her actions might lead to life or death. She would have to take charge of her fate. She threw her jacket up to cover her face and hurried past the busy man on the tractor. The wind was delivering the odorous mist from west to east. *Thank goodness, I know something about winds, directions and decision making,* Sport thought. The wind would soon carry the harm behind her. She passed through quickly.

The crisis was over, but she wondered now what other ones might lie ahead.

As Sport progressed, she saw in the valley below more smokeless factories standing like silent sentinels to mark a passing afternoon. Yet it seemed to her that the quiet facade of rural peacefulness was masking conflicts or crusades. She had a sense of people taking sides. If that were the case, she reasoned, then people might be observing her to assess her stand on things. She decided to prove that she meant no one harm and that she was neutral in their disputed territories, so she walked down the median of the highway as a symbolic gesture. She wanted to show that she was a middle-of-the-roader. This seemed to work, because occasionally a passing car emitted a short and friendly honk, as if the driver understood her mimed language of central politics.

She came upon a factory entrance sign and paused some moments to stand under it. She imagined being a worker who lived in this valley and breathed the polluted air daily. Her daydream got interrupted by a truck slowing along the right side of the road. The driver noticed her when she waved and stopped.

"Could I have a ride?" Sport called as she crossed over to him.

"Sure can!" replied the smiling driver. He seemed pleased that she would be joining him. "I watched you from way back and wondered where you were going."

"Oh, thanks! I need to get to the next town to a drug store so I can get my prescription filled before all the stores close this afternoon." She said that because she wanted to impart a sense of hurry. In fact, given her situation, she had several pressing needs. Getting into the truck would be a good first step.

Sport climbed into the cab to be greeted by the driver's extended hand. "I'm Jerry," he said. "I think we can make it." Sport shook his hand and introduced herself.

"How old are you?" Jerry asked.

For the first time in a while, Sport laughed. "Can you guess?"

His answer made her laugh more, this time in delight. "You missed quite a bit." Sport told him, and his face wore a look of incredulity.

He shook his head. "I'm usually good at guessing ages. Okay, how old do you think I am?"

She said, "Thirty-eight." It was spot on.

"Wow!" Jerry answered, chuckling. He started up the truck and put them in motion. "Well, then," he said. He paused and stroked his chin as if to indicate he was thinking about something. "Seeing as how you won our little game, would you let me ask you to dinner tonight?" His tone was that of a person who hardly knows a stranger. He sounded safe and nice, and Sport was at ease. But his proposal didn't fit in with her plans.

"Aren't you nice, but I really have to be back at school on Monday morning. I need to get a bus as soon as possible so I can get back to work."

A little more conversation revealed that Sport needed to be let out at a small town near the state line. Jerry's destinations would be taking him east. So, he let Sport out some ten miles down the road in the middle of somewhere, and Sport felt gratitude that she did not have to walk that ten miles. She parted Jerry with heartfelt thanks.

She was at a gasoline station near the river at the state line. The woman at the counter allowed Sport to use the telephone to call her bank. She couldn't get through. She only could receive busy signals and strange beeps. She would have to call later, and later seemed another hurdle.

The bus station was in the town across the river. When the obliging woman in the gas station sang out to her customers, "Can anyone take this lady to the bus station across the river?" Sport felt her heart fill with surprised gratitude. She had told Sport that it was four miles to the bridge over the river and that the bus station was on the other side. A weathered but nice-looking young man answered that he was going that way and would be happy to give Sport a ride.

She bounded into his van with him. He was affable and very soon explained his situation to her that he had become unemployed as a carpenter when business fell off. They talked about the economics of the area, and Sport suggested that he look for construction work on the coast, not far from where she lived, because there housing was booming. But she could see in his eyes that her suggestion sounded remote to him, as if the coast were three thousand miles away. He was not ready for that kind of change, she guessed.

They kept rolling along and finally came to the river, the bridge and the town. The station was on the far side of the town. Sport realized that the woman in the gas station had said the station was four miles away, but that she must have meant fourteen miles. When the station at last appeared, Sport wished badly that she had money to offer the young good Samaritan, but she didn't, so she wished him the best.

"I have had a time lately," she told him, "and you are one of just a few people to help me, even though things aren't so good for you right now. I will remember this always."

After he drove away, Sport turned to look at the bus station, and she thought that it had an ominous appearance. She shook off the feeling, because she had to take care of business, and the first was to get in touch with her bank. Was there money in her line of credit?

Again, she talked someone into letting her use the phone, but this time she succeeded in getting through to the credit department of the bank. However, the woman on the other end of the line must have had a hard day, because her tone was entirely unsympathetic to Sport's plight. She had to go to extra trouble to call another branch to determine that money might have been transferred.

"Yes," she told Sport, "The transaction was initiated on the other end, but it is pending. It came in too late to be included in today's transactions. Any charges you make won't be approved until Monday. So, you won't be able to use your card until then, not for food, lodging or gasoline."

Her tone felt like an attack to Sport. She tried reasoning with the woman, but the lady insisted in a way that seemed to Sport to be saying, "You can't go anywhere until Monday!" Now Sport understood why the bus station had appeared ominous to her. It seemed then that the woman's taunting voice was penetrating the entire station.

"I need the credit limit raised so I can get back home by Monday morning. Please," Sport pleaded.

But the woman's answer came with small laugh of indifference. "I can't help you. Those are the regulations." Then she disconnected.

Sport felt the sting of an undeserved face slap. *Why was she so antagonistic towards me?* She stood there, receiver still in hand and not able to think what the next move should be. A man needed to use the phone. Sport stepped aside, still feeling stunned, and then she felt a voice inside her tell her to listen to the intuition of one step at a time.

*Doing one thing will reveal the next.*

She had to call the school.

She waited for the phone to become available again and asked to make one more call. She dialed the school where she worked and told them that she would be back for work on Monday morning, although now she was still out of state.

*You need car keys.*

She saw through the window a Pontiac dealership across the street. Without giving more thought, she went over there to the parts department and described the car model to the older man behind the counter. He didn't answer her. He just left and went in the back and cut some keys before she could even ask about the cost. When he returned with them, she had doubts.

"I hope these fit. They look different than the ones I had," she explained to the man. Silently, he returned to the back, and when he appeared again, he had a new set. Sure enough, he had made the wrong keys!

*Luck or intuition, at least I have been spared another agony,* Sport thought. It was even better than that.

"I screwed up. I'm not going to charge you," he told Sport. She put on a look of mild protest, but he waved away an objection before she could make it. "I'm glad to have done it for you."

The truth was that she didn't know how she could have paid him, so she thanked him and hurried back to the bus station with the keys. She had bus schedules to check.

*Get a ticket to the town where your car is.*

The two ticket lines were backed up because a customer at one of them seemed to be inquiring about multiple trips. She was a pretty woman, and the man helping her seemed to have all the time that she required. Sport saw that line wasn't moving and got in the other one. By the time that she advanced to the window, the agent looked stressed and pressured by the people waiting. It turned out that the modems were down, so when Sport charged her ticket, he simply slid her card through the manual machine and handed Sport her copy of the charge ticket. By the time the transaction authorization would be run, the credit for Sport would be available. Sport had purchased a ticket to take her to the town near her car, and another to take her

93

home from there, just in case the car would not start or had been impounded. She was taking no chances on not making it back before school on Monday.

Sport breathed a "thank you" prayer when she saw the bus ticket in her hand, and she moved on. Now it seemed that she would make it home on time to prepare for going to school on Monday, after all. She went outside and sat on a bench in the docking area where the buses arrived and departed. An older man approached her and said, "It gets real hot out here, especially when the buses come. All those fumes, too. You might want to go inside."

She thought that his warning probably would be correct. Back inside the station, Sport spotted an unoccupied phone booth. The seat and the privacy beckoned her, so she sat inside it, leaving the door open for fresh air. She thought that she might take a few moments to relax and process the things that had been happening to her. She had a good view of the station waiting area. Sport thought about the past days, but then her attention got hijacked by the appearance of two small men of the same size, stature and manner of walking. They entered wearing green Mao outfits and hats. She watched them as they seemed to be inspecting the station. She thought that they were strange.

*Just what world have I entered?* Sport wondered. She wasn't thinking just of the station and the Asian men; rather, she wondered about the world she had been in the last several days. The towns she had been in should have been ordinary, perhaps dull, with ordinary people living in them. *Why did everything and everyone she had met seem so strange?*

Two buses arrived, and Sport got on one. A man sitting in the only unoccupied front seat said that he preferred to be alone. The bus was packed, but Sport headed towards the rear. Halfway down the aisle, the smell of lavatory chemicals smacked her, so she realized that it would be a difficult ride for her. She would have to look for an opportunity for a seat exchange later. Thankfully, the buses pulled into a McDonald's a couple of hours later so that people could eat. Sport's feet had been bothering her from all the walking, so she got off the bus and headed immediately for the bathroom.

The blister on her right heel looked like it could become infected and nasty. She had no bandages. She washed it off with water from the sink and a paper towel and then made a tissue

94

cushion for her shoe so it wouldn't rub so hard. At that time, three college-aged women came in. One noticed Sport's heel and said, "I've got a first-aid kit in the car. Let me go get it for you." Sport saw her as an angel of compassion and felt a tear. The girl returned with ointment and bandage. Her touch felt tender and healing.

Her friends, who had gone out, came back in the restroom and said that some men had been in the restaurant acting strangely, surveying the room as if looking for someone, but they had left and now the coast was clear. To Sport, their report seemed like a message for her. Without knowing exactly why, she felt relief.

Sport went out and filled her water cup from the fountain. She sipped slowly. The three young women ate quickly and left. Sport felt hunger kick in. When an older man and one about thirty-five came in together, she could not resist longer. She approached them before they got to the order counter.

"I'm sorry to bother you this way. Could I ask you to buy me a small hamburger? I've lost my purse. I'm a teacher trying to get home from a trip. I haven't had much to eat all day."

The young man looked at her with disdain. The older man pulled change from his pocket and fingered it as if counting. Sport knew that they didn't want to help with her small charity request.

"Never mind," she told them and found a seat again. One of the bus drivers came in, and Sport got up and asked him which bus was the best ventilated.

"Mine is," he answered directly, like he received that question often. "A lot fewer people got on mine. If you get on now before everyone starts boarding, you can claim a good seat. Just watch for your baggage when you arrive, if you have any below deck."

But as soon as Sport ascended the steps to the coach, a horrible chemical odor greeted her again. It seemed worse than the first. So, she returned to her original bus. There the man in the front seat had extended himself, napping. In the rear of the bus, Sport asked a pleasant-looking black woman if she could sit with her.

"Certainly! You can have the window seat if you need to sleep," she answered.

Sport settled in, and in a couple of minutes the bus filled and set out on its journey again. Her companion was quiet. She had an aura of peace and kindness about her, Sport thought. This gave Sport the confidence to say to her, "May I ask you a question?"

"Of course," she replied.

"Would you be able to spare me a dollar the next time we stop? I lost my purse and I am trying to get back home."

The woman looked at her with a smile, reached in her purse and retrieved two dollar bills. "Here you are, dear. I've been there myself."

"Oh, God bless you!" Sport said. "When I get home, I will be able to repay you."

The woman said, "I wouldn't hear of it. Get something to eat. I am sure that you have helped plenty of people when they needed it."

Sport reached for the woman's hand. She did it because the woman had a hand of understanding. The lady returned Sport's squeeze and smiled.

"There are so many fellow travelers in this world," Sport said, "but so few answer cries for help. But you did!"

The two got quiet again, and Sport did nod off for a while. But a loud compression sound suddenly raced from the rear of the bus to the front, accompanied by what was to Sport a horrendously offensive chemical odor. Apologizing to the kind woman, Sport moved quickly to the front of the bus and sat on the steps by the door.

"You can't stay there! What's wrong?" asked the driver, obviously oblivious to what had transpired. Sport knew that her nose was sensitive, but, surely, he would smell it, she thought. She said, "Something happened back there. Maybe there was an accident in the lavatory, but there has been a bad release of odor. To me, it is like a chemical bomb. I have bad allergies, and I can go into respiratory emergencies. I can't go back there."

The driver stared ahead, perhaps dealing with traffic on the highway or considering what Sport had told him. In the pause of conversation, the man in the front seat spoke up.

"Here, take this seat next to me."

Sport looked up at him. He was sitting upright now, an older man, and for the first time, she noticed that he had breathing tubing in his nostrils. There was an oxygen tank on the floor before him. He had not been using this when she saw him before.

While she was still taking all this in, he said to her, "Come on, it's okay. I didn't know you before, and, as you can see, I have some trouble breathing and need to hook this thing up to me. It's easier if I

96

don't have to worry someone next to me with all this. But I see that you have breathing problems like I do."

Sport gratefully took the seat. The oxygen seemed to invigorate the man and he became talkative. He told Sport that he had been traveling from Nebraska and was heading to Maine, where he might have fresh air the rest of the summer. He had a brother living there, he told her. He had been long on the bus, so he had a good handle on all that was happening on it.

"The woman across the aisle gets off at the next town," said the man. "Grab her seat when she leaves. You will be more comfortable."

The woman did exit at the next stop, and Sport moved over. She became comfortable enough to doze a while, but then an intuitive dream awakened her with a revelation that she might be near the truck stop where her car remained. She got up and knelt by the driver and tapped his shoulder to get his attention. He reclined his head towards her so that he could hear Sport over the engine and road noises. He was also attentive to the road because of a heavy fog.

"There's a truck stop before the next town where you will be stopping," Sport told him. "Can you please just pull over there a moment and let me off?"

"I can't make unscheduled stops, ma'am," was his answer.

But Sport pleaded. She told him how she had been followed, that she had to leave her car, that she had traveled by truck and had bad experiences, that she boarded the bus to get back to her car, and that she urgently needed to get home so that she could be ready for school on Monday morning.

The driver shook his head without responding, but it was a shake of irritated affirmation. He leaned forward in his seat and observed lights that arose suddenly in the fog. Sport was about to speak again, when suddenly he made a turn into a truck stop that appeared like a lit city in the fortress of fog.

"This is where you get off," he told Sport.

"Are you sure?"

"Positive," he answered, but Sport thought his tone cold and unsympathetic.

"Good luck," said the old man in the front seat.

The driver opened the doors, and the damp chill of the night rushed in. It pressured Sport to hurry. No sooner had she stepped onto the parking lot when a different chill, one of apprehension, enveloped her body. She did not think she was at the right place. But even before she could turn to rush back inside the bus, it pulled resolutely away.

As she walked across the almost deserted lot to the building, Sport took in the unfamiliarity of everything. She got inside and described to the woman at the dining counter the truck stop she was looking for.

"Honey, that's a long way from here. You are about thirty-four miles from where you want to be."

Sport felt a discouraging wave of exasperation as she turned to look out the window to the parking lot. She fought tears. Outside, the blurry halo of lights seemed like it would lose their battle with the predator fog.

And she still had not filled her prescription.

# Chapter 9: Dead End

The waitress at the counter seemed sympathetic to Sport's plight, but she didn't have authority to grant her request to use a phone, especially because a pay phone was outside. So, she passed Sport to a stressed-looking shift manager.

"We are not supposed to let the public use our business phone," she told Sport.

"Please! Just one time. I need help." Sport's face was stricken in the knowledge that she had to cover 34 miles to reach her car. "I am somewhere here in the middle of the night and have nowhere to turn and no possible way to get out of here without help. Maybe you could call the State Highway Patrol for me?"

Probably more in deference to the nice waitress, the shift manager agreed reluctantly, but she gave the phone to Sport to make the call.

"Hello," Sport began, "I am stranded thirty-four miles from my car by a bus line that let me off at the wrong truck stop. Can someone please come here to pick me up? I need to get to my car!"

"We don't handle things like this," replied the duty officer on the other end of the line.

"Please! I feel desperate. I have been through a lot."

"I'm sorry, ma'am. Just call a taxi and they'll take you where you want to go."

"But I can't," Sport explained. "I have no cash, just a credit card, and they don't accept those in the taxis."

"Wish I could help you, ma'am," the officer answered, and then he hung up.

Sport could feel the stunned look on her face like a slap.

*I have to re-group and think.*

She decided to go back into the coffee shop and talk to truckers. She approached several, but, no, none were going west. All were heading east and south. After a while, Sport became aware of herself as a lone woman soliciting men in a trucker's paradise. She became uncomfortable. Returning to the waitress, who was now busier at the counter, Sport asked advice, and the woman replied, "Go find the man wearing the blue hat."

Sport looked, and no fewer than four men were wearing blue hats. By the tone of the waitress, Sport guessed that she would be looking for the owner of the establishment. She walked up to the oldest-looking blue-hat-clad man and found that she had guessed correctly.

"I really don't like this, ma'am. What you are doing is soliciting in my place of business. No one here knows anything about you. You could be an accomplice in a scheme to rob someone. You have to think about how it looks." That was the man's response to Sport's plight!

Sport sighed and shook her head. "If that is what you think, then, please, call the city police. I have got to get out of here!"

He did. About ten minutes later, a patrol car emerged from the fog and approached slowly. To spare any scene inside, Sport went out to greet them.

The patrolman on the passenger side got out and began the usual round of questioning. Sport gave her name, address and location of her car at the truck stop west of there. She pulled the bus ticket from her jean pocket to substantiate her story that the bus driver had let her out at the wrong stop. Her coat and other personal belongings weren't with her, but they had not been stolen, she explained, so that the officers would not have to be concerned about that.

"I just need to get back to my car."

"Unfortunately, we can't transport you there, ma'am. That distance is beyond our jurisdictional limits."

That made some sense to Sport. Earlier she had realized that state police could not operate outside of their state. She asked the next logical question:

"Then can you take me as far as you can, and another police jurisdiction takes me the rest of the way?"

But Sport's creative problem solving couldn't seem to break through the tape of the local police regulations. She felt like a sole runner in a thirty-four-mile marathon. Then another idea cropped up:

In her previous marriage, Sport had been a military dependent. Perhaps there might be a military installation nearby? She didn't know, but the police officer confirmed that there was.

They agreed to take her to the military post. She got in the back seat and decided to be quiet. She realized from the conversation between the two officers that they were unfamiliar with the interior of the post and knew little about military protocol for entry. When they arrived at the front entrance, the police officer gave an explanation about Sport and asked the sentry if military police might take Sport to the MP headquarters to determine whether they could help her. The sentry stepped in his guard post and made a call.

When the sentry said that the MP would be on the way, the city police let Sport out and moved on. She stood outside. It was becoming colder and rainy, so she asked if she could come inside the sentry building. The sentry agreed. Not much else was happening other than allowing a white Camaro to enter the post.

Finally, a military police car arrived, and Sport got into it.

*I certainly have had a lot of varied traveling conveyances during my vacation days,* she thought sadly. *Some time, I will have to stop and count, but now I need to do some thinking about how to tell my story yet again. I need to insist that I speak with the senior officer of the station.*

The police car arrived at the MP headquarters and deposited Sport at the door. They presented her to a guard who brought her inside. There she was released to a young man behind a high counter. He inquired what she needed. Sport explained that she preferred to speak to a senior officer of high rank.

"Perhaps one of about eighteen years' service," Sport suggested.

The man looked at her with a small degree of wonder. "Well, you probably will have to wait until morning for that," he told her.

Sport sighed. "I don't mind waiting. That green sofa over there looks inviting, much more so than that cold rainy night outside. I know you have procedures to follow. Would I be permitted to wait over there on the sofa?"

"I don't see why not," he answered.

"Is a request for coffee pushing it?" Sport asked, daring to smile. The hope of a sofa and a warm room was emboldening her.

The coffee was a long time in coming, and Sport almost dozed off sitting upright on the sofa as she waited, but, finally, a young man appeared with more than a cup of coffee. He also had a box of doughnuts. Sport took one and suggested that he pass the others to the men on duty to share.

After the warmth of the coffee and the sugar of the doughnuts, Sport felt the day catch up with her. The comfort was making her sleepy. But knowing that a senior officer would be arriving in the morning to hear her story, she felt it would be prudent for once to be prepared to tell it comprehensively so that he might be the one, finally, to help her get back to her car. She requested a legal pad and a pen, and the young man brought her one before disappearing in the back with the box of doughnuts.

Sport began to write in sequence her experiences of the past days. There was so much to cover about her observations that it felt like she was composing some sort of intelligence report. The distractions of the front desk soon bothered her, so Sport asked if she could go the lavatory.

"I want to write. I might be there a while," Sport explained to the man at the desk. She didn't want to generate unnecessary suspicions. The young man looked like he thought it an odd request, but he nodded his agreement.

She locked the door to the lavatory and sat on the floor to write. She smiled to herself at the uniqueness of doing this. She felt warm and relaxed. Even better, she felt as if she were doing something patriotic.

*I will express my concerns for this country in my report,* she decided. *What better environment for writing something like this than a military post? It is not often that people get time and opportunity to consider their observations and think about the impact of things happening in the United States.*

So, Sport began to write from the depths of her feelings. She described the unrest in many sectors of the working society. She reported all things that were symbolic in her journey, like the cartoon with guns, the crack in the night, the red blocks, and the airplanes with triangles. She wrote about the men who had followed her, the reason why she had left her car, and the fact that she had been dumped in East Side. *And what a place that is!* she wrote. She described the horrors of her experiences there and her concern that people were like automated robots with no feeling. *What is happening in our society?* she asked. *The fabric of our American democracy is pulled and frayed.* Sport wrote her prayer that everyone would unite again in the tenets and beliefs that the founding fathers had established for our great nation. She expressed that this would now require a great amount of time, awareness and effort.

The remaining hours of the night passed quickly as Sport absorbed herself in her writing exposition, so she was surprised by the knock on the door at 7:15 am.

"Please come out, ma'am, and wait on the sofa until the senior duty officer arrives. You can watch for him there."

Sport emerged and stationed herself on the sofa. Nothing much was happening at first. A man came in who was irritated that his vehicle was blocked in its space by other cars, so he demanded that they be moved. Sport thought, *At least he has transportation, even if he doesn't have the space to pull it out.*

A few minutes later a group of about fifteen men came in and opened lockers and retrieved their weapons. They checked them, clicking and feeling them in their hands. Sport watched without flinching. *After all, I am familiar with military routine, even if I have never come this close to a firing squad.* That thought gave her a small giggle. *I am just an innocent citizen on vacation without a car and a birth certificate. Ha!*

Shortly after that, rain took possession of the morning, and Sport saw outside people running and splattering about. A garbage truck rolled up to do its duty. *Garbage day at the barracks*, she thought. It was then that an officer entered. In a few moments, a couple of guards escorted her to his office and waited with her for the officer's return. She asked them about their insignias and about the post to gain a better understanding of the type of barracks she was at. When the guards told her that the senior officer would be in shortly, she asked for a recorder to be brought. After retelling it so many times, and even recording it in writing, she only wanted to repeat it once more.

The senior officer finally entered, and Sport introduced herself to him. He nodded and asked, "And just what are your credentials, exactly?"

Sport was taken aback, but she looked him squarely in the eye and said, "I'm a citizen with rights and responsibilities." There was a podium in the room, and Sport went and stood behind it. The men looked shocked.

"Just because I'm a woman in jeans doesn't mean that I don't have public speaking abilities," Sport told them with a smile. "And in addition to that, I am a teacher, so I am quite comfortable here."

The officer took a seat at his desk and rested his arms in a body language that said, "Here I am, now talk!"

"I recognize that this is Saturday morning, and you may have been taken away from your personal time. I apologize for disturbing you, but I think we are sitting on a crisis."

He looked surprised, and he began firing off questions from his point of view that were quite out of the sequencing that Sport had recorded in her notes. She stopped him and said, "Excuse me, but I do have this report in order and I would like to proceed accordingly."

"Well, does this have anything to do with my barracks?"

"It has something to do with everyone!" Sport answered him. "Our liberty and freedoms are rapidly disappearing. We need to do something quickly."

He looked at her oddly and didn't say anything for a while. Then he asked her, "Is this a report for the FBI?"

"If you think it necessary!" she replied.

He nodded at the two guards to remain with Sport as he got up to leave the room. "I will contact them," he told her. But Sport did catch that some type of understanding passed from him to the guards without words. He was gone a few minutes, and when he returned, he said, "Two men from the FBI will be in here to interview you shortly."

He walked up to her. Sport had taken a chair next to the podium. Indicating her notes, the senior officer said, "If you'll give me your notes, I'll make copies for them so they can read along during your briefing."

Sport thought that he was acting suspiciously, but she turned her notes over to him. He returned with them a few minutes later and handed the original, hand-written yellow pad sheets back to her. He put the Xerox copies on his desk.

Then, suddenly, two police officers from the city came into the room. They were not the same as those of the previous night. The senior officer of the barracks handed them a copy of Sport's report. He told Sport that the policemen had come to take her to be interviewed by crisis intervention people at the local hospital.

*He deceived me*, Sport realized with disappointment. She fought back tears. She realized that her car was a long 34 miles away. She wondered what kind of dead end she had arrived at.

# Chapter 10: High Stakes

An intuition told Sport to go with the officers. *Freedom is sometimes seized in opportune moments,* it whispered to her.

"We're going to Siding. That's the town where the hospital is with the crisis intervention team," said one of the policemen from the front seat of the patrol car. Sport was staring out the back window at the cold, foggy morning with intermittent rain. She had already seen the sign announcing, "Siding Town Limits." It had only been about four miles from the military post. She saw a drab town that appeared frozen in time, perhaps the 1950's. All the houses were small, single ranchers with dirty, whiteboard exteriors that looked deficient of painting since the original coats. The cars and trucks in the yards were mostly fifteen to twenty years old. It was a community marginal in its income and barely holding on to what it had. Sport thought such a place might engender a significant number of personal crises that the hospital would need a team of specialists to serve its community.

"I think that there is a crisis in this general area," Sport replied. "I got separated from my car, and I have spent some days hiking in these parts and have encountered some pretty distressing things. Fear is everywhere. This is why I am going along with you. I wrote a report of my observations last night while I waited for the senior officer at the barracks. I tried to report to him, but he mentioned the FBI, and then he called you. But, maybe the people at the hospital will know what to do with this information I have, and it can be of some help. The truth is, I just want to get back to my car, which is thirty-four miles away. More importantly than that, I need to get home to Virginia Beach. That is why I need to return to my car. If going to talk to this crisis information team will help the community, I am glad to do it. I hope that afterward they will help me. I am not sure I understand your reasons for taking me, however."

"It's just that you have apparently been in highly stressful situations for days at all hours of the day and night, ma'am. These are professionals who may know best how to assist you." This time it was the other policeman who spoke.

Sport sighed. Outside, the world continued devoid of joy. She realized suddenly that she had not heard any music since leaving her car at the truck stop. *The world has forgotten its music. It has forgotten about people with simple needs. Everyone is guided by rules that do not accommodate, and they have too much fear to look beyond those rules. Time and money required and rules are the dictators of effort to help others. Where is love?*

She did feel weary again. She wondered how much more interrogation she could endure. She had experienced one crisis after another, moment by moment, inch by inch. She wondered if she really was any closer to home. More tribulations might still lie ahead of her, she realized.

*I've been reactionary in my moments of problems, and I haven't taken time to pray! I have good instincts about times to trust and times to be cautious, and I've relied on those, but forgetting to pray is low-level performance on my part! I know I have divine protection, but I shouldn't take it for granted, or, surely, I will be handed lessons to learn. Maybe that is why all these things have been happening to me! For things to get better, I need to be on my game with endurance, faith and courage.*

When they arrived at Siding Hospital, the officers got out and opened the door for Sport. Inside, off the Emergency Room entrance, they found a room with a door having a sign that said, "Crisis Intervention." Sport thought, *Well, isn't this nice?*

The officers went off, leaving her with two young women who introduced themselves as crisis counselors. Both were working on their Masters in Social Work. They were the staff for a Saturday morning of crises in Siding. They started with the predictable questions, and Sport went along with direct and basic answers long enough to realize that these young ladies would have no idea how to assess the report of observations that she had taken time to write. Therefore, when it seemed to Sport that they had learned enough about her to realize that she was sane, she decided to move the conversation to a higher level while she still had her tired wits intact.

"You know, we are all equals here," Sport said. "I have my Master's degree, and you are working on yours. I see no need to tell you my story and have you evaluate it as good or bad. I know what it is and what I am doing. What would you like to talk about? Do you know about Bloom's Taxonomy or Maslow's Hierarchy Theory?"

They knew about Maslow but not Bloom. So, Sport inquired about their study programs and made suggestions about what they might want to research and include in their theses. She became the teacher and they the surprised students.

Sport asked for a cup of coffee. One rummaged deep in the desk drawer and produced a tea bag, which Sport thought was fine. Then, since she was at a hospital, she asked whether her sore and bruised feet might be washed and bandaged? She expected that they would accompany her to the emergency room for this, but, instead, one of them kindly washed and bandaged her feet there. The other went for extra gauzes in the emergency room in case she might need them. Sport tucked these into her jeans pocket.

Now the social workers did not seem to know what to do with Sport. So, Sport pressed and asked if one of them could take her to the bus station. She had lost hope of making it back to her car before Monday. It seemed that the universe had rebuffed all her attempts to do that. She had had more luck with the buses. She felt an urgency inside her to get home so that she could take care of her job and negotiate arrangements to return to get her car. She just wanted to be home!

The two young women whispered uneasily between them. They asked Sport to show them her bus ticket. One went quickly to the emergency room to see how busy they were and then returned to say it was quiet. They came to an agreement that things were slow enough that one could drive Sport to the bus station in town and would hurry back to the hospital.

"I'll pull the car up," the young social worker told Sport when they emerged outside. To Sport's surprise, she drove up in another New Yorker, a dark blue, older one with blue plush fabric seating. Sport got in the car with a sense of relief that she was on her way again. The girl was silent, the car seemed to float on the road, and Sport fought sleepiness so that she could look out the window and observe the town of Siding.

*It is a strange place*, she thought, as she noticed that several very wide streets in this small town were one way. *What would be the need for that?* she wondered. Despite the town's seeming simplicity, the young driver was having a hard time figuring out how to get downtown at every intersection of choice. She didn't live in the town. Finally, they found the bus station, a small brick building. In her enthusiasm to be free and on the road, Sport shook the hand of the young woman and thanked her quickly. She got out, but before she closed the door, she noticed something odd.

"I don't think the station is open," she told the girl as she observed the lack of people and cars and the dark appearance of the building.

"Go check," said the young woman. "I'm sorry, but I really need to get back. I could be in trouble for being away, and it has taken me too long to bring you here. If there is any problem, see if someone will help you get to your car." With that, she reached across the expanse of the New Yorker's front seat and pulled the door closed. Then she was on her way!

Sure enough, when Sport walked up to the station door, it was locked and all was dark inside. She saw a weathered bus schedule posted on the brick front wall near the door. The print was fading, and it was even worse for reading in the mist and rain through Sport's weary eyes. It showed a couple of buses a day departing on Tuesdays, Thursdays and Sundays.

*How could there be no bus on Saturday,* Sport wondered with incredulity. *Of all the days in the week, certainly there is a Saturday bus,* she reassured herself. *This is some old schedule that no one bothered to replace.* The buses departed at 10:20 a.m. and 2:30 p.m. on the scheduled days. That would mean that she would have to wait about three hours.

She almost believed that the bus would come. But then her intuition screamed loudly to her: *No bus on Saturday!*

Sport looked around at the buildings nearby. Everything looked closed. She sighed and strolled down the street. A couple blocks away, she saw a small downtown diner that she entered from the soggy mist. She heard some noises of occupation in the back. Otherwise, there was no indication of people. She sat and waited at a table. She had a few moments of being glad to be out of the chilling weather, but then she realized that no one was aware of her presence in the place. She got up and called to the back, where earlier she had heard noises. But no one came. She left, closing the door gently.

*Strange place, this little town of Siding,* Sport thought. *It truly seems off the main line of living.*

Outside, no one was in sight. She didn't want to die of cold and starvation! She thought of her own hometown and what would be open downtown on a Saturday morning. Restaurants and diners, of

108

course. A hotel. A police station (*no thanks*). The library. The thrift shop.

*The library! Aha, that's it! It would have phone books and directories that I could use.*

She walked to the corner and took an intuitive turn to the left. A block and a half farther appeared an old building that would meet the criteria for looking like a library. She hastened her pace to the steps of the building, and from there Sport saw that the lights were on inside. She entered, and in the vestibule was a beautiful, lit showcase filled with children's art and crafts. She saw fingerprints of love all over the pieces.

A librarian was at the main counter. Upon Sport's request to use a phone book and telephone, the woman cheerfully affirmed that she had those for Sport. Sport quickly thumbed through the yellow pages to the church listings. She had thought earlier on her walk that maybe a pastor might be willing to drive her the 34 miles to her car. Seeing a familiar-sounding church name, she dialed, and with good fortune, for once, the pastor answered. Sport introduced herself and explained that she was stranded in his town and really needed his help. He introduced himself and told her that he would come to pick her up at the library.

"I'm not far away," he added.

Before going out front, Sport returned to study the showcase. To her delight, she saw that inside were letters from children in Russia asking the children in Siding to pray for peace. They wanted peace, not war! They signed their names, and then Sport saw answered letters signed by the children of Siding.

*Thank God for the innocence of children*, thought Sport. *They may be our only hope.* The display gave her a better view of Siding. *The universal plea of children right here in this town!*

Shortly, a young man walked in and verified that he was the pastor with whom Sport had spoken. He had a compassionate look about him, so while they stood in the vestibule of the library, Sport unloaded much of her story and her current situation of still being stranded. As the story wound on, the pastor gestured with his arm that they might proceed outdoors to his car. But when Sport began to recount her problems with smells that made her sick and the need for fresh air, the pastor halted.

"I was going to suggest that we come back to my church office and talk and figure out how to help you. We're very busy today. The service is tomorrow, and I'm still preparing my sermon. We're printing bulletins. I have an old mimeograph machine being used by the office assistant, and I am afraid that the chemical odors from that are pretty bad. I can barely stand it myself."

Sport felt a bit of deflation in her hope of a pastoral rescue. "Is there any possibility that you could take me to my car? It is 34 miles from here."

The young man shook his head. "I'm just out of time. I'm afraid I can't do that." He paused for a moment, thinking. "Look, let me take you to the Police Station."

"Oh, no! Not again!" Sport protested in exasperation. "They won't help me. I 've already tried to get them to take me. Everyone acts like something is wrong with me."

The pastor asked her a couple questions about the police station that she had been in, and then a look of understanding lit his face.

"I'm talking about a different precinct. I know the officers there. I work with them sometimes in helping transient visitors. I know someone there who will help you. Let me take you so I can get back to work."

A bit leery, Sport agreed and got in the Pastor's mini-van, and off they went to another police station. He led her inside and asked for a specific officer. When that man came out, the pastor gave him a brief explanation of Sport's presence. Then he made a quick apology to leave, and he was gone.

Sport looked at her new interventionist. He said to her, "Let's go to this back room." He seemed like he would be dealing with her in a normal fashion, so Sport didn't feel a hesitancy about complying. She followed him down a hallway until he opened a door to a room at the end and made a polite gesture that she enter first. The room was a small lounge with vending machines and a table with some plastic-backed chairs.

"Have a seat," he said. "I'd take a chair facing the door. I am going to shut it. We are about to bring a very bad man by. If you don't mind waiting just a few minutes, I will be back. May I offer you some coffee and soup? It will be good for you."

At first, Sport declined the soup, but then she learned that it would be chicken noodle soup. She remembered that when one doesn't feel too well, chicken noodle soup had almost magical, curative powers. Maybe it would be the sustenance that she needed to make those 34 miles to her car or to survive a bus trip home.

"Yes, please," she answered.

"Good," the man said, and then he left, closing the door behind him. She did hear activity of people walking in the hallway moments later. She kept quiet.

He returned as promised with soup and coffee. "I called my wife," he told Sport. "We live close by, and she is going to come in and talk to you to see if she can help you or take you somewhere."

Sport couldn't believe it. Someone had responded to her stated need with kindness. Before the soup and coffee were gone, a lovely blonde woman in blue jeans, cloth jacket and pretty blouse came into the room. She introduced herself as the young officer's wife, Susan.

"I try to help my husband out with errands that he would like to get to but can't because his job keeps him so busy," Susan explained. "He asked me to take you to the big city."

*The big city!* Sport thought. *This is a kind lady.* She thought about her options. If she asked Susan to take her to her car, there was the possibility that her car would not be there. Given her luck on this trip, Sport changed her assessment to high probability that her car would not be there. Even if it was, she didn't know if she had enough energy to drive home. She chose to ask Susan to take her to the bus station.

During their drive to the big city, Susan asked Sport if she had any money.

"No," Sport replied. "That has been my big problem. I have never had an opportunity to get to a bank, and my credit card will not have additional funding until tomorrow night."

Without flinching, Susan put her hand in her pocket book beside her and fished out her wallet as she continued driving. She passed Sport ten dollars to see her through. Then she talked about the city and the surrounding area to give Sport more of a flavor of what it would be like to live in that area.

They stopped first at a brick bus station with red shutters beside the windows, but that wasn't the right station for Sport's ticket. They drove a few more blocks to the right one. Susan came in with Sport.

"I just want to be sure you are in the right place and get on the right bus before I leave you," she explained.

The ticket agent told Sport that the next bus to her town would board in about three hours. Sport didn't mind that. The station felt warm and cozy, and she could sit and watch people. She said goodbye to Susan with a hug. As Susan walked away, Sport wondered whether she would ever see her again.

Sport went into the restroom and washed her face and combed her hair with her fingers. She didn't have a comb or makeup, but she still had a small tube of lipstick in her pocket. She dampened her hair to give it a wild and wet look. She liked the look, and the cold water felt wonderful on her scalp. It seemed to liven her brain cells. They had not had much rest, she realized.

Returning to the terminal to find a seat, she heard an announcement saying, "Last call for Washington, D.C." That was where she had to go to change buses to make it to her hometown. Sport hurried to the man standing on the platform beside the bus and told him, "But I was just told there wasn't a bus for three hours!" He looked at her ticket and then smiled. "Nope. This is your bus. Get on, let's go!"

She might have worried that the weirdness was starting again, but Sport got on and nearly collapsed into a seat. Later, if someone asked her what seat she took, she would laugh and say, "I don't remember!" Somewhere between the big city and Washington, D.C., the world faded away and Sport slept. Every once in a while, she roused enough to notice that she was on a bus, but then she succumbed to irresistible slumber paced by the hum of the tires on the road. Her electrical current was off. Of those miles and hours to Washington, Sport remembered nothing.

But she revived when the bus rolled into the station and the driver announced loudly that everyone would have to change buses. Sport dreaded the business of overcoming her inertia to get off, find the right gate for the next bus and wait in line. It had been a long time since she had changed out of that purple blouse and jean suit. They might have fit her figure well. Sport presently felt numb and doubted that she had any kind of figure.

She got off the bus and looked around. The driver said, "There will be a forty-minute layover here." But the departure time he announced didn't match the forty minutes that he had indicated. *No one seems to understand time schedules,* Sport thought. *I'm just going to have to be careful and observant so that I don't miss my bus.*

She felt in her pocket for the ten-dollar bill. She remembered that she had given it to a young man to buy her a pack of crackers sometime in the early evening. She fished out the change and decided to get something to eat. Having so much money made her feel very blessed. She ordered a serving of mashed potatoes and gravy and a little bowl of lima beans. The vegetables were not well seasoned, but they were warm and did not take long to eat. She sat observing the other passengers and located the new bus driver, who was finishing a sloppy meal. He had a beat-down and preoccupied look, a countenance that did not inspire her confidence in trusting her life to him. She would keep an eye on him to be certain that she did not miss her last connection home.

Getting up from the table, Sport found a seat near the door through which outside breezes darted in upon every opening. Each gust tussled her hair in a touch of gentle refreshment. Getting the oxygen that she needed had been a problem for her the entire trip, she realized. Always in life, this had been a concern for her. Sometimes she felt as if the entire planet lacked the few thousand oxygen molecules that she seemed to require for a comfortable respiration.

The driver finished eating and went out to the bus platform. Sport followed him just as the announcement blared through the speakers that it was time to board the bus for her destination. Moments later, the thick of passengers for the bus log-jammed at the door. Some sort of change in air pressure seemed to lock the door, and the people closest banged on it and pulled and pushed. Sport shot a look at the driver. He had a smile of condescending amusement on his face.

*Wow, it's clear he doesn't like his job or his customers,* thought Sport with concern.

The passengers managed to get the door open just as the fuming exhalations of the buses outside began to give Sport a sickening feeling. She saw that the driver had chosen the bus and had taken his seat. She rushed to board to get ahead of the coming crowd and select the seat that she wanted.

The bus filled with the bumps and coughs of humanity, and, after what seemed like an hour, finally pulled out and nosed its way through the streets of Washington, D.C. Through the window, Sport saw the big limos that transported people to Saturday night parties. The lovely ladies dressed in formal wear reminded Sport of the times in which she used to do elegant things. Those seemed so long ago, the hats, heels and long dresses lost to the past. The bus pulled onto the freeway, and Sport exhaled a big sigh.

That sigh awakened her to an environmental reality. She became conscious of a chemical odor permeating the bus. Adding to discomfort was the fact that the packed bus had become warm from the packed bodies generating heat. The summation of the two quickly felt suffocating. Sport got up and approached the driver.

"We have some bad smells back here, and it feels very stifling," she told him. "Could you please turn on the air conditioner to give us some fresh air?"

He looked back at her with annoyance. "You don't need cool air. It's getting cold outside. It's my responsibility to keep the passengers warm." He glanced back and noted Sport's shocked look. He seemed to get some satisfaction from that, and he put on a smile, but it looked like a cruel smile to Sport. "Please return to your seat," he told her. "It's not safe for you to stand near me. It's against regulations."

As she returned, she saw that many of the passengers were already sleeping and others looked droopy-eyed. The bus had become much quieter. The chemical smell was stronger. It was the odor of lavatory chemicals much more intense than should be normal, Sport thought. She had a premonition.

*I don't dare go to sleep and lose consciousness of what is happening around me*, she warned herself.

Noting that the old couple across the aisle from her already were sleeping so deeply that they appeared comatose, Sport took her seat and remembered the gauze in her pocket. She took it out and poured some water on it from a water bottle that she had brought onboard. She certainly hoped that this would be a solution to work. She applied the gauze to her face and breathed moist air into her nostrils. This was a blessing. It was filtering out the putrid odors that were starting to give her a headache. She settled into a realization that not only did she have to stay awake, but she needed to do something to keep her wits about her. She wanted a mental activity to keep her from panicking.

So, looking out the window, Sport waited for the mile marker, and then she counted seconds until the next one. Her game would be to estimate miles per hour that the bus traveled. They rushed by in under a minute, and as the rural night grew darker, the bus clearly accelerated its pace. Sport then watched for the sign posts that gave distances to the next town. But, as time went on, she felt overly warm and dream-like. She started thinking about relativity, and the mileposts seemed to rush by even as the sound of the bus on the road sounded like it was moving slower. She shook her head several times to dispel sleepiness, and, once, when the urge to sleep was especially strong, she forced herself to pour more water on her gauze and then breathe through it deeply. Even so, she suspected that there were moments when she was not present in the realm of the awake, and when she looked at the passing mileposts, some of them looked curved, as if they were bending under the blow of a gale of light.

The bus was crawling, but the signs whirled past. She saw one whirling by that reported her destination to be 34 miles away. The irony of that number startled her. She became more awake, and she reached for the nearly empty water bottle so that she could freshen her gauze.

That was when she noticed what the driver was doing. He was driving with his head near a cracked-open window vent so that he could take in fresh air as the heat and the chemicals built pressure inside the bus. His nose inclined towards the vent while his eyes peered straight ahead to the road. Suddenly, Sport could feel how powerful was the force of the blowing heat of the bus. She anxiously glanced around to the side of her and behind her. The old couple across the aisle slumped lifelessly in their sleep. Behind her, everyone was deep and far gone. She wanted to shout.

But when she looked to the rear of the bus, the rush of chemical odor overcame her. She had not been covering her face with the gauze. She saw the suffocation coming like a black tsunami. The images of the passengers began to spin in a circle in front of her eyes like the faces of the dental staff had done when she was a child and the dentist had given her gas to put her to sleep. She fought desperately to keep consciousness, but she knew that she would lose.

With all the strength and will power that she could muster, Sport pulled herself around to look at the driver. The faint dashboard cluster lights showed clearly his head inclined against the pane of the window vent and his closed eyes directed straight ahead. The bus crept to a stop, and the thick dark fog of toxins outside passed through the windshield and overcame Sport with its blackness. Just before the end, Sport glimpsed brightly-lit-flower fields and sniffed honeyed breezes in a flash of home that beckoned from a different age and place.

# Section 3: Resurrection

# Chapter 11: Connection

Sometimes Sport thought of it, the awful journey of disconnection that had come to such a discouraging end. When she remembered, she saw Christa's face at that moment in which Christa had recognized that her earthly dreams of space travel and future teaching were shattering into pieces high in the Florida sky. How was Christa to know that her inspiration and example would keep her alive in the hearts of students and a grateful nation? Sport always felt very thankful for the company that Christa shared with her when they made that trip to Monticello so many years earlier. To Sport, Christa McAuliffe lived for the children and because of the children.

*She rode with me because I am the same*, Sport decided. *She knew I would keep her secret.*

Who would keep Sport's secret? It was one that Sport let herself accept, but slowly.

She couldn't deny the memory of the second birth canal trip. Memory? For years, it seemed more like random impressions in her mind that came at odd moments, like in the middle of the night when they could be confused with dreams; or in times of emotional excitement when tears were mounting; and even during her practices of detached meditation when she tried not to have any thoughts at all. These were not simply memories or involuntary creations of imagination. No, Sport *felt* the journey. It was wet, squeezing, urgent and moving. She was blind and warm, and, suddenly, out in the damp, dark cold.

About fifteen yards from the bus.

Her instinct was to run and get back inside, but why? She had pushed the door open. She didn't remember this until many years later. The news reports from the beginning had described it as a murder-suicide that took place just thirty-some miles from her home. She would begin to read those stories, but always she stopped. She had given herself permission to release herself from the horror of reading it. She was in a different condition and did not need to experience base curiosity any longer. Then one day she remembered.

Before anyone arrived at the scene, Sport pushed the bus doors open and rushed up the three steps to stand beside the slumped-over driver. In the darkness, she discerned the lifeless bodies of the passengers. Her eyes moved to the seat where she had been. She knew that she would see herself.

She was there.

Within milliseconds, Sport saw the faces of children that she needed to reach through generations into the future. The pain of her absence from them was too much to bear. She saw the faces of them change when they learned that she was not coming.

*No! I see all the days when I want my students to feel the joy and excitement of learning about themselves! Who would approach them with a zip and zing of enthusiasm that will radiate their personalities?*

Sport rushed to the seat where her body was and commanded it to awaken. Lights from a car approaching from behind began to illuminate the bus through the windows. The distraction startled her, and when she looked again, she saw that Sport was not in her grasp and not on the bus. She hurriedly darted through the doors and into the dark, thick forest.

\*\*

The first five years after the incident seemed to her like a repeat of childhood amnesia. Sport didn't remember much of that time thirty years later. She had shot out of the second birth canal all ruddy and red-headed and full of spit and determination. She felt a Scot kinship again. She melded it later with her first history of Scottish ancestry coming to Virginia. She finally made it to the school that Monday. She never breathed a word about being on the bus. Someone commented to her that she looked refreshed from her days off.

They had been a nightmare. Sport went running to the teacher's lounge bathroom mirror. She saw her skin liquid and glowing and her red hair dark and thick. Despite the memory lapses to follow in the busy years ahead, Sport would always remember that encounter with her reflection. In those moments, she remembered the warmth and pressure of the second birth.

She worked in a couple of school systems in Virginia through the years, and always the children of special needs and gifts drew to her. Sport loved them, but she also looked out for the parents who had special anxieties for their children. Some were difficult, but most saw how Sport had a unique tuning for each child. Consistently, Sport garnered praise and popularity among them and the staff.

As years wore on, parents and teachers noticed something strange about Sport. She heard it in whispers and saw it in curious or admiring or jealous glances.

"She hardly ever seems to age. She looks almost like she did thirty years ago."

This she heard from chaperone parents going on school trips with her and the kids to Monticello, and at concerts and plays and performances given by the students. She saw it herself when she washed her face in the mornings.

*What miracle is this, Lord?* Sport would ask. Inevitably, the answer sprang forth in the memory of last night's dream: She visited unearthly, beautiful cities in the heights of mountains that dwarfed those of her Appalachia. She met beings who spoke in languages that could not have been Latin-based, and, in her dreams, she understood them. The skies sometimes had stationary space stations so big and close that they could be seen in the daytime like the dull white moons. And the sounds! She felt the sweet musical vibrations of birds and flying creatures winging at incomprehensible speeds. In those dreams, she saw night fall, and the stars came on like kisses caressing her body.

"Hello, stars in space!" she sometimes sang out. Then she would awake feeling energized and young.

One morning, she became determined to build a space station, and she would get the kids to help her. It was a perfect idea for a trans-generational project. Each child in her tutelage contributed ideas, essays, research and working models to one of the five spokes of the station. The spokes were centers for work in science, technology, engineering and math (which years later became known by the acronym, "STEM"). Sport reserved the fifth spoke of activity for something close to her heart; namely, radio astronomy. She wanted ears listening for her "astral ancestors," as she joked with the students. Only, it was never a joke to Sport, and many students delighted in choosing the spoke of their teacher's heart for their focus of learning and contributing.

*Energy transference.*

That is what Sport felt around her special students. Their excitement and innocence electrified her, so that she worked tirelessly for years to let NASA and the scientific community know what her students were up to. They had ideas for a space station laboratory that would be international and thought out by young people who would be parents or grandparents by the time their extraterrestrial construction might be seen as a faint star in the night sky thanks to reflected sunlight. With every class, the models and research projects, drawings, high-concept-ideas and treatises accumulated. This started in the early '90s, and Sport meticulously maintained a room and catalog of her students' work. In later years, some of her technologically adapted students moved the catalog to school computers, and videos of students explaining and demonstrating their projects got added.

Then the money started to come in. The first fund at school found contributors from parents and bake sale activities. This hardly covered expenses.

But Sport and the children began inviting scientists from nearby NASA in Langley and professors from fine Virginia schools to attend science fairs and be keynote speakers at PTA meetings, and some of them found money to contribute or suggested foundations to tap. When parents and school administration noticed this, they upped the ante, and programs at the school featuring "The Space Station" became more seriously funded. After a while, in the region where the school was, any reference to "space station" first was understood to be this one by Sport and the students.

Sport learned to write grant requests. She needed a 501(c)3 organization, and, along with the principal, took the issue to the school board and charmed them into an approval for a Space Station Foundation. Sport became the enthusiastic, youthful-looking champion for special needs children who could envision their future in space and in a better world where their ideas would be recognized and valued.

The years whizzed by like a satellite in orbit. Sport taught students in grades six through eight. Some were gifted, some had special needs to be accommodated, some had been considered ordinary, but Sport intuitively brought out the best of their intelligence and aptitudes. She flew high with them on wings of aspiration. The days came when she began teaching children of former students, and she knew that she was close to seeing even grandchildren. The middle school students went to high school remembering the space station and Sport. They were delighted when

121

Sport agreed to substitute occasionally in the high school and they would be reunited with her some days.

The foundation money grew. One of its funds began accumulating quickly. That was a scholarship fund for college education. Grandparents of students were dying and leaving scholarships in their names. When the year came that a former student showed up with her grandson to meet his new teacher, Sport, the foundation funds had grown to over eleven million dollars.

It had been thirty years since the bus incident, and Sport looked maybe 48 years old at most. She felt even younger. She thought about the space station nearly every day. She remembered the ones in the daylit sky in her dreams. She had infused the heart-thrill images of those in the minds of all her students. When they worked on their projects, they took them to that space station in their own skies. Sport focused most of her personal time considering studies that elaborated the fifth spoke, where the computers for the radio telescope resided. She saw its giant receiver constructed above the outer flat side of the station and held in place by the connector tunnel through which the astronauts could float to make adjustments and repairs to the disc. She brought the reality of present-day to the listening bowl through tireless research into the ever-surprising discoveries of the radio telescopes on earth. She was certain that before she died, there would be contact with civilization on planets outside our solar system. She had an intuition within her that the beings would already be aware of her.

The pain of her experiences in that middle life of the road trip, when she felt beat down by all the disconnected souls, never left her. She had been an every-person for a while. She thought that her trip of homelessness and abandonment and ultimate bus ride were some sort of divine mechanism to reveal to her the condition of souls of people on earth. When she needed help, the few people who tried to assist her fell short, but many would not help her or could not.

*They were afraid. Paranoid. Slaves to rules and regulations. Helpless. Dependent on technology that they couldn't understand. When they looked me in the eyes, they didn't see me. Some wanted to use me. In the end, one wanted to kill me. And why?*

She shot out of the second birth canal wet and fierce and full of spirit to help people. For reasons that she only partly understood, she knew that she had been spared a dreary continuation of what she considered her "previous life." What she could do for people would require generations of time, and she would start with the children. The special children. The ones who could intuit. The ones who could make people yearn for a higher purposed life if they had opportunity to shine. She felt grateful for the revelations coming to her. She had almost let planetary life beat her into the submissions of resigned thinking and abandonment of hope.

*Where did I come from?* She thought of angels, but they seemed beyond the grasp of her mind as opposed to planetary aliens. Still, she wondered sometimes: *If in God's great heaven there are no genders, just angels on high, is it possible that angels fall to this planet by choice or design? If they fall to human dimensions, is gender their choice?*

Sport thought of angels when she felt her loneliness. The men she considered soul mates had always been married and her arrival on the scene too late. The very fact of feeling so connected to them, a mutual feeling or not, sometimes made her wonder about angelic origins. *Love has varying weights,* she thought. *The heavier, earthy ones become ensnared in passions and conditions. The lighter ones lead to happiness rarely felt. A yoke of love is light when shared for life and surprising when the path's beginning leads to unexpected destiny. The happiness of fortunate couples derives from enjoying life that is spinning always and there will be no need to fall in love again. Two natural hearts combine to one supernatural.*

Her men on opposite coasts or the ones slaying dragons held dim positions of affection now in Sport's heart. In her re-birth, she acknowledged the men attracted to her, but she brimmed with love for her students, the ones like angels holding her hand up the path to the heavens.

Like the arch-angel, Tommy. She met him in her sixtieth year. He was a sixth-grader who rarely spoke and never made eye contact. Sport suspected that he used his autism as a wall to hide his brilliance because he didn't want to bear the responsibilities that came with that. He liked being social zero. But his writing skills betrayed his genius to Sport. She observed him carefully, looking for the weak entrance to his defensive heart. In the classroom, when Tommy became anxious (for always unpredictable reasons), he would release a torrent of words as loud as spring thunder and continue them in sporadic bands of charged protests. Rocking in his seat, he made the other students uncomfortable, and they laughed nervously. This only provoked shame in Tommy, and his anxiety increased. The barrage of words burst forth like machine gun bullets until, unexpectedly, there would be total silence. Then Tommy would stare at the ceiling and rock, totally unresponsive to Sport's gentle comforts.

Parent's Day approached, and the students were to give little speeches on topics such as what they wanted to achieve this year or in life, why they loved their parents or country, what interesting thing they did the past summer, or whom they wanted to help in the world. The important thing was the exercise in public speaking more than the topic. Sport knew that she would need to help Tommy with this, so one afternoon she arranged to have a few minutes alone with him at the end of the school day.

"I'm not going to do it," Tommy proclaimed to the ceiling. "No one sees me. They just want to laugh." He rocked in his seat.

"Well, of course no one will laugh, Tommy! But I bet you that everyone will want to hear what you have to say. It is because you are so quiet. They are curious about you."

"No! I don't want them to know. I have secrets."

Sport pulled a child's chair next to him. She was petite enough to sit on it comfortably. "Everyone has secrets, Tommy. Some good, some bad. Are you afraid of your secrets?"

"No. I tell them." He became quiet.

"Who do you tell them to?"

He didn't answer. Sport tried to move her face to his field of view, but he looked away. She decided to let the silence remain a few minutes before pressing on. But he was the one to speak first.

"I know who you are," he said loudly to the ceiling.

This surprise confused Sport momentarily. "Good, Tommy, I am your teacher who loves you."

"I mean something different." He turned his face towards her, still not looking her in the eyes, more to the side of her eyes. Then he looked at the ceiling again. "You got off the bus."

It felt like a smack, and Sport saw in her reflection in the window the uncertain and stunned look on her face. She waited, and when Tommy didn't say anything else, she asked him, "What bus, Tommy?"

"You know, the bus. You were in the shoot of light. You got back on the bus. Then when people started to come, you ran into the woods."

For the first time in years, Sport felt the lack of oxygen. She fought a feeling of panic. Tommy turned and looked to the side of her again.

"It's okay," he said. "You have secrets too. I never tell." He rocked.

Sport managed to force whispered words:

"Tommy, how do you know about this? It was many years ago, before you were born."

"Yes, but I do research on you. I like you," he answered loudly. "I found the story, the bus crash. Then I remembered my dream all the time, when I see you get off the bus."

Sport felt tears coming. *I am not going to cry in front of Tommy!* "I don't tell anyone about it, Tommy, because I don't understand it. I can't remember it well. I only have impressions in my memory. I barely remember the woods, and I don't remember getting home. Tell me about the light."

He was quiet for several seconds, then he blurted to the ceiling. "It was a line of light, very fast. Then you stood up out of it. You looked all wet. Then you ran on the bus."

Sport couldn't speak. She allowed them both to be quiet. After several minutes, she asked, "You said you tell your secrets, Tommy. Who do you tell them to?"

"I talk on YouTube," he responded. "I talk to the camera. It doesn't make fun of me."

Something clicked in the back of Sport's mind. "Can I see you on there?"

"Yes, I talk like you sometimes."

Her eyebrows raised with that one. "Tommy, let's go look now. You show me, okay?"

They went to her computer at a small table in the back of the classroom, and Sport signed them on. Then she watched as Tommy confidently took his place in front of the screen and signed into YouTube with his user name and password. He was "Starship Tom." Sport was shocked at what she saw. Tommy had his own YouTube channel and had uploaded nine videos. There were no subscribers to his channel. When he talked, he stared directly into the camera and spoke in a normal voice. He sounded matter-of-fact and calm, and it was the first time that Sport ever felt like Tommy was looking directly into her eyes.

"I will play you this one," Tommy told her. He moved the curser over to a clip called, "My teacher."

"I talk like you in this one."

Sport watched as the video loaded. There was Tommy, apparently sitting at his bedroom desk. Looking into the camera, he announced, "This is for my teacher. I think she might be an angel. This is how she speaks: 'There, sitting on my desk, is a little angel that seems always wanting to spread its wings and fly. It must have descended from heaven above and fell on my desk. Wow, this might catch my students' brilliant thoughts! Good morning! Let's bow our heads for a moment of silent prayer. We will place no boundaries on our requests!' But I interrupt the teacher, and I say to her, 'Can we just ask God to tell us what is important for us to learn today?' (I asked her that once.) And she said, 'Oh, that is so beautiful! So why don't we each take a place of an angel and give our names as 'The Angels Speak?' Then we bowed our heads and raised a prayer: 'Dear Lord, just tell me who I am and why I am here?'"

The video continued, and, again, Sport felt like she might cry, but she didn't want to set Tommy off, especially now when he was sitting so calmly with this technology. She focused hard, and then she said to him, "Tommy, you are so good in front of the camera! You look right into the lens. It seems like you are peering directly into my eyes! This is excellent what you do here!"

Tommy kept his eyes on the screen. "I talk to people through my camera," he said. "I don't like to look at them when I talk in real life. It is just the way I am."

Sport reached over and put her hand on top of his, even though she knew that he would not respond to the gesture. "Tommy, I have an idea. What if on Parent's Day we do this: When the classmates give their talks, maybe you could give yours by talking into my camera? You could sit at a desk in front of the room, and I will sit in a chair in front of you and film you with it? You can make your speech to the camera. We can explain to the class and parents there that you have a YouTube channel and that I thought it would be a good idea to record it and upload it."

Tommy didn't hesitate to answer. "I can do that. I don't want to talk to the people."

"I know, Tommy, but when you talk in the camera, you will be talking to people, and they will want to know what you have to say."

"Yes," he said, and there followed a long silence. Sport sat quietly thinking about Tommy's dream revelations. How could he really know about the bus? Should she think that the "shoot of light" was real?

Then, as if he could read her mind, he said, "You weren't supposed to leave us. That is why you are here. You won't leave until your work is finished. I am not going to tell anyone what I know."

Sport sighed. "Tommy, tell me, what is it that you want to do when you grow up?"

He didn't answer then, but he did on the night of Parent's Day.

The students had given their reports, the parents and the faculty there had clapped, and the optimism in the room was palpable. Sport had been her effervescent self, praising each student when they concluded and keeping the atmosphere light and amusing. When it was time for Tommy's report, she announced that she would be filming Tommy's talk for his YouTube channel. This brought some applause and surprised, "wows," from the audience. When Tommy's parents saw this, the anxious looks that had been on their faces relaxed, and they smiled a little as they glanced around the room.

Tommy got up and went to a table set up for him in the front of the room. He rocked in his chair and shot looks to the ceiling. But when Sport sat in her chair, pointed the camera at him and said, "OK, Tommy, we are ready," he looked directly into the lens and began a confident patter.

"My name is Tommy Brisbane," he said, "and tonight I want to thank my classmates and especially my teacher, Ms. Sport, for all the patience that everyone shows to me in class. I have autism, and I do not relate to people or situations in ways like most others. But I want you to know that I hear everything, that I see how smart my classmates are and that many teachers in this school want us all to do well. People have asked me what I want to do in life. Ms. Sport once told me that I should enjoy life by pursuing my dreams. But it is not a dream for me. I just have something that I will work to do. I want to be a doctor. Especially, I will be the doctor on the space station that we are building. All the people who have worked on this a long time, thanks to Ms. Sport, all the students and everyone else, have been building a future for themselves. We have been learning how to get things done. I know there is a lot of money for the space station and it will take much more. But it will take me ten years to become a doctor, and maybe by then, the space station can be built. If it takes longer, I will help, but the people who will live on it will need a doctor, and I am the first to say that I want the job, so I will get it."

This brought laughter from the audience. Sport could feel that something magical was happening. She didn't want Tommy to become distracted, so she kept the camera steadily on him, and he never wavered from looking into its lens. And then, as she watched the viewing screen, she imagined Tommy standing in a white lab jacket on the space station while making an announcement to people on earth.

"Ms. Sport will have a job on the space station, too," Tommy continued. "She has been listening for other civilizations in the stars for a long time. I see her there, sitting at the computers, and the look on her face when the first broadcasts from another world are detected. She will be excited and happy, and maybe she will even think that the beings contacting earth are her family, too. Ms. Sport will care about them. She teaches us all to care about each other and to talk to each other. I haven't been able to do that before, but Ms. Sport found a way, and tonight I am here talking to you. I think that everyone here, if they want to do something smart, they will ask Ms. Sport how they can help get our space station built. Well, thank you."

There were cheers and applause. Sport gently lowered the camera, got up and went to the desk where Tommy was sitting. He stood now, looking a bit to the side, but when Sport said, "Tommy, I am going to give you a little hug," he looked directly into her eyes. He didn't smile, but he did stiffly accept her hug.

"You don't have to wonder, Ms. Sport," he told her. "You won't go home until your work is done."

That night Sport lie in her bed watching the night sky through her window. The night was crisp and fresh, and Sport let the breezes blow on her body. For the first time, she felt a peace inside her about her life. She had beings looking out for her, she knew, be they angels, God, or aliens. She would never understand or know, and it didn't matter. What mattered is that hearts touched. She saw that the sky was brilliant with stars. While she watched, a meteor blazed a four-second swath so bright that it seemed to slice the night in half. It dropped below the horizon, as if it were a spaceship that found a landing area just beyond the field of view. Sport felt in her breast the thrill of a lover's kiss. Then a broad smile crossed her face.

"Hello, out there, stars in space!" she said.

The End

# About the Authors

 M. J. Scott (U.S.A.) is a country girl who has climbed mountains, has placed her bare feet in all fifty states, and has lived a life of unique expression of joy in personal and professional endeavors. Marilyn studied education at Manchester College, earning her BS in Education and following with her MA in Mass Communications at Norfolk State University. She completed all but her dissertation in the doctoral program of Education Administration at California Coast University. A retired gifted-students-teacher, she began her career working at Dr. Albert Schweitzer Elementary School in Anaheim, California. Later she spent 20 years in education in the public-school systems of two Virginia cities. In more recent years, Marilyn has had a photography and video business and has done philanthropic work. In 2015, she became co-founder of The Writer's Council, an organization serving to encourage aspiring writers to achieve their dreams to become published. Prior to her publication of her first novel, *Sport's Alien Fantasy*, the author published four books dealing with personal and spiritual fulfillment and travels of earth and awareness.

 *Sport's Alien Fantasy* was first written by M. J. Scott in rough draft form in 1986. Her editor and publisher, Daniel Wetta, recognized the extraordinary story within its pages and corroborated with her to show its relevance to today's digitally connected world. The authors and the publisher believe that global connections and disconnections so prevalent in our lives currently had their beginnings in the mid-1980s. Because of this corroboration, Sport found a new beginning and ending. She lives to be, perhaps, the extraterrestrial being who can teach us what we need to know to master living and loving one another on our stressed planet. More can be known about Daniel and his books, publishing, editing and marketing services at www.danielwetta.com.

www.ingramcontent.com/pod-product-compliance
Lightning Source LLC
Chambersburg PA
CBHW071314130626
46556CB00004B/1600